Inspector

The Lady from Rome

John Tallon Jones

TABLE OF CONTENTS

CHAPTER ONE

It was just after eight in the morning, and Visco was finishing his second cappuccino. Even though it was only the beginning of May, it was hot. Mrs. Visco was making pesto sauce by the open window and enjoying the sun on her face and lean, already tanned body. She ground the pine nuts and mixed in garlic and olive oil and the aroma filled the room.

"I don't think you need a jacket today," she said. She had come to this conclusion by observing people passing by the villa. They were walking slowly as if the hot air was a solid wall that they had to break through. They tried to keep in the shade and complained, in an overly Italian way, about too much sunshine.

He was in the middle of eating a cornetto when the telephone rang. He walked over to the window, picked up the receiver and also surveyed the scene outside. The white villas shining in the bright Southern Italian sun hurt his light blue eyes. He pulled down his

Gucci sunglasses that were fashionably perched on his head and scanned the sky for clouds. He couldn't find even one.

"Hello? Is that you Visco? It's Roberto here from Potenza."

If Chief Inspector Roberto Felici was calling his home this early, it must be something serious. Felici was his boss and knew that Visco treated his breakfast like a religious ceremony. He didn't like to be disturbed until, at least, his third coffee. "What is it, sir?"

"I'm sorry to bother you at breakfast, but I think you need to drop everything and concentrate on a problem that has just come up. Have you much on?"

"Nothing that can't be put on hold."

"There has been a murder. I only got the news ten minutes ago. It took place in Maratea. Do you want the address?"

Visco picked up a pencil and pad off the telephone table. "Go on."

Well, it could be a murder or a suicide from the information I have been given. The body was found by a cleaner. The lady in question, who is dead, is named Marina Ferro."

"Where in Maratea?" Visco scribbled the address down on the pad, tore it off and put it in the breast pocket of his shirt. Roberto began to talk again, but now Visco wasn't listening anymore. His boss did tend to talk too much. He waited for a natural pause for breath, said, "I'm on my way," and put the phone down. He wasn't being rude; he was in a rush to get to work.

Mrs. Visco was waiting at the door with his lunch box and a flask of chilled sparkling wine. He was smiling as he left the house and started up his black Alfa Romeo. He loved the south, and he loved his job. Murder was something that had always intrigued him. He hoped that it wasn't suicide.

The streets of Maratea were already full of people. Locals were opening their shops and erecting market stalls, and tourists were drinking coffee in the fashionable town square. The beaches would also be filling up soon and later on in the morning; the local restaurants would be preparing the exquisite fish dishes that the small town was famous for.

The address was in the more affluent area of town and set apart in the hazy, smoky mountains. He pulled up outside an apartment block that was about ten stories high and already buzzing with police activity. Nothing much happened in Maratea and the residents of other apartments and villas had gathered on the street corner and were gossiping knowingly about what they thought had happened. Of course, nobody actually knew, but Italians liked to talk and speculate, and it was better than doing the household chores.

A policeman was guarding the entrance.

"Which floor?" asked Visco.

The police officer threw down his half-smoked cigarette and ground it into the floor with his boot. He looked embarrassed, and blurted out. "Top."

He strode through the entrance and was immediately overwhelmed with the coolness and marbled eloquence of the lobby. There was a man in a light gray uniform sitting behind a desk watching TV. The man watched him walk past but didn't get up or challenge his presence. Most people in the region knew Visco, as he had grown up locally and was related to many of the townsfolk. The old-fashioned cage lift worked noiselessly and had probably been installed for effect rather than to save money. Inside there was a plush red carpet, which was an unusual item to have on the floor in the south.

When he reached the third floor, he made his way into the apartment with the door that was open. Inside was his assistant, Luca. He was talking to another detective and look relieved to see him.

Visco walked over and waited for Luca to explain the situation.

"I've not touched anything. I thought that you would want to question the cleaner. The doctor has briefly examined the deceased and left about ten minutes ago to get his breakfast. He will be back later.

"Where is she?"

"Follow me; she's in the sitting room."

On the floor in front of a huge window overlooking the bay, a blonde haired woman lay on her back. The area around her head was covered in blood, and there was a deep dark slash under her chin. "She was stabbed once in the throat and fell backward," said Luca.

"And the cleaning lady?"

"The cleaning man is in the kitchen."

The two men entered a state-of-the-art kitchen. A man was sitting by a huge dark oak table, looking into space. He had fair hair and blue eyes. He looked up with disinterest at the two detectives now towering over him.

Visco sat down next to him. "What's your name?"

"Hugo Berlinski."

"German?"

"Polish," said the man defensively.

"Would you like to tell me in your own words what happened."

The man's face expressed no emotion or fear. He spoke with a slight East European accent.

"I arrived here at around seven o'clock. I usually do the cleaning while Marina is in bed. I hardly ever see her, and she leaves my money on the kitchen table."

"So you have a key to the apartment?" asked Visco.

Berlinski nodded and continued. "I heard the TV in the sitting room and saw that the light was on so I popped my head around the door, and saw her lying there. I didn't touch anything and immediately phoned the police."

"So how long have you worked for Marina Ferro?"

"About twelve months. Why is there a law against it?"

Visco ignored the remark. "How often do you come and how many hours do you stay?"

"I work from seven until nine and don't come at the weekends."

"It's a bit unusual for a man to do cleaning work. Do you clean anywhere else?"

"Sometimes, but I don't have anything as regular as this, and now I don't have anything regular at all. In Poland, I am a plumber, but here you must take what little work you are offered."

How long have you been living here?"

"Ten years." He added. "I married an Italian."

"And the name of your wife?"

"It was Gilda, but don't bother, she ran off with a Turk and now lives somewhere in France."

"So if you didn't go into the room, how did you know that Marina Ferro was dead?"

"It was obvious from the blood."

"What did you do while you were waiting for the police to arrive? Did you alert the neighbors or talk to the security man downstairs?"

He shrugged and glared. "I sat down and waited. I leave all of that to you. It's not my fault that she is dead."

"So you never touched anything while you were waiting?"

"No."

"You didn't see a knife?"

"Definitely not."

Luca interrupted. "We are searching for the murder weapon at this moment."

"What sort of a person was Marina Ferro?"

"How should I know, I barely spoke to the lady. As I said, she was always in bed when I was working here."

Visco got up, pulled out an enormous handkerchief and wiped the sweat from his forehead. It was already very humid and would get worse towards midday. "Do you have any idea who might have done this?"

"The only idea that I have, inspector, is that it wasn't me. Can I go?"

"You can go after you have answered me one last question. Did she have any boyfriends or anybody she saw on a regular basis?"

"I'm only here for a couple of hours and have never seen anybody in the apartment except her. There are some clothes belonging to a man in a wardrobe in the spare room, and in the bathroom cabinet there is aftershave and an electric razor."

"Do you have any idea who the man is?"

Hugo shook his head. "The aftershave is expensive, and so are the suits, so he must be rich."

Visco nodded. "OK, you can go, but give your details to my assistant and don't leave the area. I will more than likely want to speak to you again.

He went back to the sitting room where the men from forensics were waiting for orders to start the process of ripping the apartment apart.

"I want a full report on my desk no later than tomorrow morning, Luca. I'm going down to talk to the man on security. Do you know if it is twenty-four-hour coverage?

"There is just the man that you saw when you came in. He comes in at seven and leaves at around ten at night. He doesn't come in on Sunday.

"So that's a no." Visco made his way to the entrance and shouted back over his shoulder. "Don't forget to get some men searching the grounds for the weapon, and keep those nosy neighbors as far away as possible."

He took the stairs down to the ground floor in the optimistic hope that the killer had thrown away the murder weapon on the way down. The security man was still sitting behind his desk and still watching TV. The only thing that had changed since Visco had arrived was that now the man was smoking a cigarette and drinking coffee.

"Good morning, sir."

"Good morning, Inspector."

"So you know who I am?"

The man drained his coffee and nodded.

"Unfortunately, you have the advantage of me. What's your name?"

"Filippo Pardo."

"And are you aware what has happened here, Filippo?"

"I gave one of your men a coffee, and he told me that Marina Ferro had been murdered. Is it true?"

Up close, the doorman's uniform appeared slightly shabby and stained with food. The man was in his early thirties and looked as if the job he was doing bored him.

"We aren't sure what happened at the moment, it could have been suicide. Did you know her well, Filippo?"

The man looked startled by the question. "I didn't know her at all. She wasn't like the others, though."

"How do you mean?"

"Well, she always said hello and wasn't such a snob."

"Did she have visitors?"

"Sometimes." Again, he looked nervous.

"Is there something that you are not telling me about the lady?"

Pardo avoided eye contact and tried to sound calm. "Why do you say that?"

"Because you seem to be a bit uneasy. Are you uneasy, Filippo?"

"No, why should I be. I do my job, go home and keep what goes on in the building to myself."

"Was there anything particular going on with Marina Ferro?"

Pardo shrugged and pretended to go back to watching the TV.

"We could have this conversation in the police station. Is that what you want?"

"She didn't have that many visitors. In fact, it was just the one. A man."

"What sort of a man? Did you ever speak to him?"

"No, he wasn't as friendly as her. They went out together a few times, and he usually arrived in the evenings."

"Did he stay the night?"

"This is not a prison, inspector. The tenants are allowed to do what they like."

"Did you ever see him leave in the morning?"

"He occasionally did."

"What about this morning?"

"I didn't see anything this morning, but he was here last night."

"Did you see him leave?"

"He hadn't left when I went home at ten."

"Do you have a name for this man? For instance, is there a book for visitors to sign in?"

Pardo found this amusing. "There is no book, inspector.

"Did she have any other visitors?"

"No, nobody that I saw."

"What time did this man arrive?"

"Around nine o'clock."

"And is the door locked after you leave?"

"Yes."

"So it is a likely conclusion that if the doctor estimated the murder took place between nine and eleven o'clock last night that this stranger did it. Wouldn't you agree?"

"How should I know? I just work in reception; I'm not paid to catch murderers." He added, "Not on the money that they pay me."

"So is there anything else that you can tell me about this man. I am assuming that he was Ferro's lover. Can you describe him?"

"Good looking, tall, dark hair and arrogant."

"That would just about cover most people in the South of Italy, Filippo. Is there anything specific that you remember about him?"

The man thought about it for a moment. "Only that he was not the sort of person I would like to have had an argument with."

CHAPTER TWO

"Between nine and the early hours of the morning, roughly speaking," said the police doctor. They were sitting in Visco's rather cramped and hot office, along with Luca.

"Was death instantaneous?"

"As you could see from the knife entry wound to the throat, it was probably not instantaneous. Death occurred due to asphyxiation after about two minutes. She would have lost consciousness before then. Whoever did this must have hated this woman."

"Or had a vicious temper and had been made angry by something," said Luca.

Visco looked at his assistant. "So what exactly are we looking at here, Luca?"

"Well, I don't think that it was a crime that involved burglary, though we don't know if something has been stolen. We asked the cleaner to have a look around to see if anything was missing and he seemed to think that everything was in order."

"So we must conclude that this was a crime motivated by something that happened."

"Or passion," said the doctor. He got up from his chair, closed his briefcase and headed for the door. If you don't need me anymore, gentlemen, I have work to do.

Luca went into a beige folder, took out a printed card in a small plastic bag and slid it across the desk. "While we were checking we found this." The card said Happy birthday and was signed Dario. "This was in a box with a pair of red stilettos. They must have been a gift. Could Dario be the boyfriend?"

Visco turned the card over in his hands thoughtfully. "Have it checked for fingerprints. If we are lucky, it will come up with something. Anything on the victim?"

"Quite a lot actually." Luca took a sheet of paper out of his file and began reading. "Marina Ferro has a criminal record. She has only been living in Maratea for just over twelve months, and before that, she was in Rome. She has had a suspended sentence for prostitution and was known to have been a pretty big earner on the call girl circuit. Mainly with visiting wealthy Arabs and Americans. She was busted by undercover agents and got away with a two year suspended sentence, for giving the name of her pimp. He was later arrested and was sent to prison."

"Revenge killing?"

"That's a possibility, but the man in question has only served three years of an eight-year sentence."

"So what we are saying, Luca, is that a known call girl from Rome has moved to Maratea and is living in a luxury apartment. Do we know why?"

"It all points in the direction of a mistress. We have looked at her bank details, and she doesn't appear to be paying any rent, and there is very little money in her account. It is possible that she owns the apartment though this is still not clear."

"So where did the money come from? Does she have a job?"

"None that we can find."

"What about the man's clothes and shaving gear?"

"The shaving gear is expensive but untraceable. The suits, on the other hand, are designer. The label is Vittone, which is made locally. We know where they were bought from, as it is a very small but expensive fashion outlet."

Visco got up from his chair and picked up his sunglasses. "So what are we waiting for? Let's go and pay them a visit."

The fashion house was on a nondescript side street tucked away in the tiny village of Aieta. There was no sign above the door that gave any indication that inside the building was a high-quality tailor. Upon entering, the two men followed a long dusty corridor and entered a room that had no windows but was cool because of a noisy air conditioning system. There were five women at work behind antique sewing machines and in the corner; a man was cutting cloth on a table with a guillotine that looked deadly sharp.

On the far wall, there was a rickety wooden stairway leading up to an office that had a window at the front, which gave a perfect viewing point to watch the women at work. Visco and Luca climbed the stairs and entered without knocking.

A small middle-aged man was sitting behind a mahogany desk writing in an old ledger. In the corner of the room, a young woman was hammering away at a typewriter. The man looked up and scowled, but his expression changed when he saw Visco's ID.

"Police?"

"Would I be correct in thinking that I am addressing the owner?" Visco smiled, and the man visibly relaxed his aggressive manner.

"Davide Vittone at your service. To buy an original Vittone will cost you a month's salary, but judging by what you and your colleague are wearing, it will be worth the expense."

"I'm here to get some information, Mr. Vittone."

"It's a shame, for the police, I could do you a very sweet deal."

Visco looked out of the window at the scene down below him on the factory floor. "Are all of your workers registered for tax?"

"Of course, inspector. What is it that you want to know?"

Luca passed the images of two of the suits over. "Do you know who you sold these to?"

"Why of course. I know these suits as if they were my babies. Some of my best design work and only good enough for somebody of celebrity status."

"Such as?"

"Such as Fabio Conte."

"What? The politician, Fabio Conte?"

"Exactly. Politician, playboy and TV celebrity. Only such a suit is worthy of such a heroic Italian."

CHAPTER THREE

It took only five hours for forensics to come up with a name after they had examined the card for fingerprints. Dario Barone was a small time crook who had served time in prison for car theft, drug dealing, and pimping prostitutes. The fact that he lived in Rome tied him firmly to the murder victim, Marina Ferro. The fact that using call girls for financial gain was one of the latest crimes he had been punished for put him at the top of the list of prime suspects. Along with a full report, Visco had been sent a prison photo of Barone. He was an ugly looking character with a shaved head, pockmarks on both cheeks and vacant dark eyes. Visco could see why the man on security had said that he was a person he wouldn't have liked to argue with.

It was Luca who had been given the job of tracing Barone, and he carried it out in his usual logical and efficient way. It was near midnight when the telephone, in Marina Ferro's flat, rang for the first time since her murder. A detective, who had been assigned the duty of packing clothes to be sent away for examination, answered and remained silent.

"Is that you, Marina?" The voice on the other side didn't seem to be overly suspicious of the silence. He added. "Are you with somebody and can't speak right now. Is it him?"

With the lack of an answer, his suspicions began to get aroused. "Is this 0985 72456?"

The detective could hear the man breathing heavily down the line. Music and mainly male voices in the background told him that this was a call from a bar. At last, whoever it was hung up. Within five minutes, the call had been traced to a bar in the town of Scalea, which was situated on the coast in the bay of Policastro.

Luca took the half hour journey to Scalea and had his driver stop a little distance from the bar. Even at one o'clock in the morning, the streets still had tourists heading from discos to bars that were dotted along the seafront. The Piano Bistro had most of its outside tables full but was empty inside apart from a couple of drunks nursing drinks at the bar.

The owner realized that Luca was police before being shown his ID. He recognized the picture of Dario Barone and confirmed that he had been in earlier. He also confirmed that he was a regular visitor for breakfast and had used the phone before he had left.

Upon leaving the bar, Luca glanced up the street at a rundown hotel called the Metropolitan. This was well known to him, and most of the police in the area, as a hangout for prostitutes and drug dealers. It was just a hunch, but sometimes these paid off. If Barone took breakfast in this bar, then there was a good chance that he lived nearby. The Metropolitan suited his profile perfectly. He walked in and confronted an old woman sitting behind a reception desk. She sniffed the air as he approached as if she could smell the police.

"What room is Dario Barone in?"

"First floor, room eleven. But he's out."

"Are you sure that he hasn't come back yet. He left the bar he was in over an hour ago."

"He's out," confirmed the lady. "Can't you see the key to number eleven is still on the hook?"

Luca showed her his ID. She didn't look shocked but lit up a black cheroot that smelt vile.

"What do you want him for?"

Luca ignored the question and hit back with one of his own. How long has he been staying here?"

"About a year. He pays regularly and doesn't cause us any trouble." She added under her breath, "Until you walked in."

"So how long does he usually stay out? Does he come back the same time every night?"

"I don't spy on my guests."

Just then, a fat middle-aged man came down the stairs with his arms around a young girl in a skimpy mini skirt and low cut blouse. When they saw Luca, they hurried out into the street.

"Maybe we should do the spying for you. I could always put a call in and have some of my men come and interview your guests. Is that what you would like?"

"He is usually back by now."

"Does he stay here alone or with somebody else?"

"Alone, but he has a lady who visits sometimes"

"Just the one?"

"Her name is Marina. Beautiful looking girl, and by the look of her very wealthy. She is always dressed eloquently and the stones that she wears look pretty authentic to me."

"Was she here yesterday?"

"No, but she was last week. I remember because I served them coffee in the TV room."

"Give me the key to number eleven."

She shrugged but looked genuinely concerned. "I give you the key, but don't wreck the room and make it obvious that you have been in. If you do, he will blame me."

Luca went into room eleven, which was a small single with cheap furniture, no bathroom and no view of the beach. The bed was traditional iron and on the bedside table, was a plastic box containing a toothbrush and shaving gear. There was dirty washing draped over a stool, and a few old clothes hanging in the wardrobe. It was in the drawer that he discovered along with several pairs of men's underwear, some fancy lace black stockings, a black basque and a casket containing jewelry. Unless Dario Barone was a practicing transvestite, these items must belong to a woman, and Luca guessed that the woman was Marina Ferro.

On Visco's desk at police HQ there was a lunch box containing ham and mozzarella sandwiches and a glass of Prosecco. Visco listened patiently to his assistant as he ran through his efforts at tracking down Dario Barone.

"Have you got somebody to watch the hotel?"

"The hotel and the bar where he phoned from. At the end of the street, there is a club called the Blue Anchor."

"I know it," said Visco.

"I am going to try it when it opens tonight. It may be nothing but the place is full of prostitutes and drug dealers, it could be just the sort of environment that Barone would hang out in."

"We've been trying to close that place for years. Until the commissioner of police decided, it would be better for us to keep it open and have undercover people inside. That way we could keep an eye on the low-life."

"I think that Barone will have made a run for it and is half way to Milan by now."

Visco took a bite of his sandwich. "On the other hand, if he is innocent and doesn't know that Marina Ferro is dead. He would still be hanging around."

"His sort has an inherent mistrust of the police; I hope that I can catch up with him tonight."

The front of the Blue Anchor was painted an understated dark purple. It was eleven o'clock on a busy summer evening, but the club looked deserted. Nightlife in most of the South didn't get going until after midnight. Inside, the main room was large and filled with plenty of shadowy cubbyholes for the low-life of the town to make drug deals, and hookers negotiate prices. It was well known that the upstairs bedrooms at the Anchor were not used for sleeping, but nothing had ever been done about it for years. The club had a slightly run down atmosphere now, but when it was newer and better run, in the 1960s, it was a place frequented by only the best girls and many notable members of the town hall and police department.

A bald headed man in an electric blue Zoot suit and mauve brothel creepers was eating a dish of pasta with a heavily made up middle-aged woman who had seen better days. He didn't look up from his bucatini and tomato sauce as Luca approached, and cleaned his mouth with a large white handkerchief before he spoke.

"What do you want? We are not open for at least another hour. Come back then, and you'll be well looked after."

Luca produced his ID, and the owner leered and stuffed more pasta into his mouth. Up close, he had a gray skin complexion and a boxer's nose. He looked as if he hardly ever got any sun on him. The woman got up and disappeared through a door behind the bar. The man went through the same cleaning routine, then threw his handkerchief down dramatically and pushed his plate away.

"Go on." He sounded bored.

"Are you expecting Dario Barone in tonight?"

The man made a play of looking around the room in an exaggerated manner. "Unless he is hiding under a table, he is not here now. I'm not a clairvoyant, how do I know who comes and goes in my club?"

"So was he here yesterday?"

"Why? What has the poor bastard done?"

"Possibly nothing, but I need to ask him a few questions.

"Questions about what?"

"About Marina Ferro. She is his girlfriend or rather was."

"What are you saying? What does was mean?"

"Because Marina Ferro was murdered."

Unless he was a very good actor, the man looked genuinely shocked. "When was she murdered?"

"Yesterday evening. Was Barone here yesterday?"

The man nodded. "He was here for a couple of hours. Don't ask me when he arrived or left because I would be lying if I told you that I knew."

"What about her? Did she come into the club much?"

"Occasionally. They would come in together. She never came on her own. They would have a dance, listen to some music; the usual thing."

"Did they have many friends here?"

"Not that I recall. They generally kept themselves to themselves. How was she murdered?"

"Let's just say at the moment, that she was murdered."

"Not by Dario Barone."

"Did I say that? I never indicated that we suspect him. We only want to talk because he is obviously an interested party."

The man examined his fingernails. "So is that it? I need to have my dessert."

Luca dropped a card on the table. "If you do see him tonight, tell him that it is in his best interest to come in and see us. This is my number if you have any information to give me."

The man didn't pick the card up. "I'm sure that one of your men will be able to tell him personally as you will, of course, be having the club watched."

"It is in your interest to cooperate. As a club owner, I'm sure that you don't want club inspectors to come and regularly visit to see how many people you employ on the black and how much drug dealing and prostitution goes on."

"I'll keep that in mind."

As Luca headed back to headquarters, he had the feeling that his threats had not been taken seriously and that the owner of the Blue Anchor would already have telephoned Barone and warned him that he was wanted for questioning. It was a simple rule of the south that low life looked after their own kind and didn't respect authority.

CHAPTER FOUR

Visco was still in his office when Luca got back. He looked as cool and calm as usual, which in the circumstances amazed his young protégé. A roof fan whirled noisily at full speed and merely succeeded in pushing hot air around the room that was thick with the stench of sweat and stale wine.

Luca passed on the information about his attempts at finding Barone.

Visco listened patiently, and then picked up his notes to brief his assistant on what had happened since he was away. "I've circled copies of Barone's picture to all local police and carabinieri. We have a good chance of picking him up if he doesn't decide to hide."

"I have a man watching his hotel and also the Blue Anchor club should he show up there."

Visco picked up a green file. "This is the full information that has been sent to me from Rome, about Marina Ferro. She has led quite a colorful life. She was arrested at the age of thirteen for asking men for money in return for sexual services. She spent much of her teens in and out of institutions for young offenders. At eighteen, she went off our radar. There is an interesting snippet from when she was twenty-two. She was picked up during a raid on a party, at a well-known mafia boss's home in Naples. While several other girls were charged with prostitution, Marina got off with a caution. She seemed to have friends in very high places."

"Or just the one friend in a very high place, sir."

"I was coming to that. While we don't have any connection between Marina Ferro and Dario Barone, they were both in Rome at the same time. They were both involved in the call girl racket, so we can assume they must have known each other. We know about her being busted in Rome and getting a suspended sentence after giving the police the name of her pimp. She was twenty-five at the time. Two years later, she arrives in a luxury apartment in Maratea."

"Strange," mused Luca.

"Not half as strange as who owns the top floor and terrace of the building."

"Fabio Conti?"

"Correct. He lives there with his wife, who is fifteen years younger than he is."

"So what's the next step, sir?"

"Well, Conti certainly ticks all of the boxes. He's got money, is a well-known playboy and has an eye for a pretty face. It's definitely not boyfriend Barone paying."

"Yes, but with his wife is in the same building, isn't that a bit obvious?"

"Yes," agreed Visco. "We also don't have any proof that he was paying the rent on the apartment. We still don't have any details about who owns the place."

"What about the other apartments, sir?"

"We are checking them now and interviewing the owners. A lot of them are summer places, so we are having difficulty in getting in touch. One or two live as far away as Turin and Venice. Oh yes, I almost forgot. I received another report from the police chief in Naples. That friend in a high place we were talking about earlier. He sent me a list of all the guests present at the party that was raided. Top of that list was Fabio Conti."

It was early the next morning when Visco drove along the coast road to Maratea. The sun, although low in the cloudless sky gave warning of another blisteringly hot day with ninety percent humidity. He was glad to be out of his overheated office, and he was full of enthusiasm for the day ahead as he pulled up in front of the plush apartment block and got out of his car.

The doorman was sitting behind the reception desk drinking coffee and reading a football magazine. It was cool in the building and quiet, with the only sound coming through the open window of the sprinkler system spraying water on the garden.

Filippo Pardo looked up from his reading and took his glasses off as Visco approached. He didn't acknowledge the detective but took a sip of coffee and put down his journal.

"More questions inspector?"

Visco leaned against the desk and produced a notebook. "Why? Are you too busy to assist me with my inquiries?"

"Always on hand to help the police. So she was murdered, then?"

"Well, unless she stabbed herself in the throat and then hid the knife."

Pardo seemed to find this funny. "It's not very often anything exciting happens here. Fire away with your questions, though I don't know very much about Miss Ferro."

"So are you sure that you told me everything that you know when we spoke before?" He saw the man avert his eyes.

"Why ask me that?"

"Because in my experience, I know when somebody is hiding something. Call it my detective intuition, but I get this feeling about you. Did you have any input when she signed the contract to rent the apartment?"

"No, because that's not my job."

"I need to find out how Miss Ferro acquired the apartment, but nobody seems to have any idea. Is she renting or did she buy it?"

"I don't know. Like I told you, this is not part of my job."

"Then I must interview everybody in the building to see if anybody knows. I think this morning; I will go up to the top floor and start my line of questioning there. I will tell them I have spoken to you."

This time Pardo looked genuinely worried. "The top floor? Why start there?"

"Because that is the apartment that belongs to Fabio Conti and his wife, isn't it?"

"That's right."

"Do you know if they were at home on the night of the murder?"

"Mrs. Conti was, but her husband was out."

"Was she at home all day?"

"Yes. Her mother came for a visit and stayed late. I had gone home, and she hadn't left."

"So when did Mr. Conti get back?"

"I haven't got a clue. He certainly wasn't here before I went home."

"Is he often out late?"

"Yes, he works very hard and is also asked a lot to go on TV in those political chat shows that are always on. I find them very boring to listen to."

"So are they both at home now?"

"He left to go to work before I arrived. I know this because his car is not in the car park. He probably will not be back until late. She hardly ever goes out, so I think that you will find her at home."

"Then I will go and talk to her."

He had almost reached the lift and was about to open the door when Pardo called him back.

"Inspector Visco!"

Visco had been expecting it, and he turned and walked back to the reception desk.

"Do you want to tell me something about Fabio Conti?"

"He didn't kill her."

"I never implied that he did. I do think that he has something to do with her apartment, though. Am I right?"

He was silent for a few seconds as if he was mulling it over in his mind what to do. Finally, he nodded with a reluctant look on his face.

"And your reason for not telling me before?"

"You never asked, and besides it is only an opinion. I have no proof.

"Does Mr. Conti pay you to keep quiet?"

"No, but he got me this job, and I owe him something for that."

"Like loyalty?"

Pardo looked away in embarrassment. "I suppose that you could say that."

"Loyalty goes out of the window, Pardo, when it comes to somebody's life. What about Mrs. Conti?"

"She knows for sure, but I guess that she is used to it."

"How do you mean?"

"The whole building knows about it. Ferro wasn't his first mistress and won't be his last."

"If he killed her, then he won't be in any position to find another lover."

"Don't you read any celebrity magazines, inspector? There isn't a week that goes by without a picture of Fabio Conti with some gorgeous young girl. If his wife was jealous, she would have given him the push by now."

"How would you describe Conti?"

"He was sixty-five years old last month, but still has the energy of a teenager. I only know that because I read about what he gets up to. His wife is never with him."

"What's he like as a person?"

"I obviously don't know him socially, but he always says hello, and he has done a lot for the area. Some of it with his own money."

"And you are certain that he didn't meet Marina Ferro the night she was murdered?"

"The only person I saw going up was the man I told you about."

Visco had heard enough and headed back to the lift."

"Are you still going to see Mrs. Conti, Inspector?"

"Since Mrs. Conti knows all about the affair. I think she will be expecting a visit, don't you?"

As the lift door closed, he heard the sound of a radio come alive and being tuned to the local news station.

CHAPTER FIVE

"So this is all she has to show for her life?"

"I found it in her bedroom at the back of the wardrobe, sir."
Officer Bruno was the only person left in Marina Ferro's apartment
and had been finely sifting through her possessions. There was a
silver shoe box with a red bow on the lid. Bruno had emptied the
contents onto the table and was meticulously looking at each
individual item. The jewelry was cheap, and the few ornaments were
the sort that would be found on a market stall. Marina Ferro's knick-
knacks didn't include a passport or anything fancy. The stuff that
was arrayed around the apartment looked like it had been bought for
her by a rich admirer, but Visco concluded that the story of the real
Marina was in this small box. These were the things that she must
have brought with her from her previous life. They were sparse,
chipped and fragile; a bit like the woman herself.

Her birth certificate had been issued in the coastal town of
Civitavecchia in the province of Lazio. Her father was Paulo Ferro
who was a mechanic and her mother Claudia De Vuono, who had
put her job down as a babysitter. There were several black and white

family pictures and a peeling silver crucifix, plus a letter from her mother, informing her that her father was seriously ill in hospital.

"We need to check the family out, Bruno. You can get onto it right away."

Bruno put his jacket on, but before he had a chance to reach the door, the telephone rang and startled both men. Visco picked it up. He didn't say anything but listened.

A woman's voice said. "May I speak to somebody in charge, please?"

"This is Inspector Visco speaking. How may I be of assistance?"

"This is Ana Conti speaking. I believe that you are coming up to see me."

"How did you come to that conclusion?"

"I have just spoken to Filippo Pardo. I was on my way out, and he told me that you were in the building and wanted to talk."

"So where are you now?"

"I am in reception."

"I never heard the lift."

"I don't like lifts, inspector. I always take the stairs. May I come up and see you?"

"Wouldn't it be easier if we meet in your place?"

"My husband would not be pleased about that. May I come up to see you?"

"OK, if that's what you want."

Two minutes later, there was a knock on the door. Visco opened it and stepped back.

"Come in Mrs. Conti."

She walked in and walked straight through the small hall and entered the sitting room. She was small and mouse like and could not have been any more than her mid-forties. She was expensively dressed and wore her hair in an unfashionable bun. Visco noticed that it was streaked with gray and that she wore no makeup. This was obviously a woman who did not feel the need to present herself unnaturally to the world or had given up trying. She didn't waste any time on niceties, which was unusual for an Italian.

"I wanted to talk to you about this awful business. I would have come to the police station because my husband doesn't like strangers in our home."

"Do you always like to carry out your husband's wishes?"

"He has a certain position that needs to be respected, so yes, I do."

Visco had noticed that she seemed comfortable in the room and had not taken any time whatsoever to glance around. He wondered if she had been here before. "When was the last time you were in this apartment, Mrs. Conti?"

She answered cleverly. "These apartments are all the same. Ours came with the furniture, and I am assuming that so did this one. It is hardly a palace, and besides, we have graver things to discuss than room designs."

"What about your husband? Has he ever been in this apartment?"

"I think that we both know the answer to that question, Inspector. I won't insult your intelligence by lying."

"Go on."

"We have been married for twenty years, and right from the beginning, Fabio has been perfectly honest with me. That was one of the reasons why he married me. He has never hidden anything from me because he doesn't have to."

"So you are telling me that you have an open marriage. Does that work both ways?"

She laughed at this. "Fabio devotes his life to people. He is something very rare in Italy, an honest politician. That's why he is so popular. He devotes his life to his work and has helped so many people that you will never hear a bad word against him. He sometimes works eighteen hours a day, but no man is perfect, and my husband is no exception."

"I'm not sure that I understand."

"Have you got time for me to explain?"

"Fire away."

"Fabio comes from peasant stock and what he has achieved with his life is down to sheer hard work and willpower. It is also because of the women that have always tried to protect him and help him. First, it was his mother, and then...." She let the sentence drift off as if she was trying to put into words something that a mere human like Visco could understand. "He has this certain quality that makes you want to mother him, but like a cat, he can't be loyal. When he was younger, he was stunningly good looking, and he has never come to terms with being old. It has given him a certain attitude. Average people like you, inspector, would never understand."

"Try me."

"Well, to put it crudely he is a sex addict. That is, he cannot stop thinking about sex and is like a stallion amongst a herd of frisky mares. He can't resist. In his day, no woman could resist him. I include myself in that."

"So he has been unfaithful to you, and it doesn't bother you?"

"The first night that I met my husband, I was with my friend Angela. He got us drunk and bedded the two of us. We had that threesome relationship for a couple of weeks until he got bored with Angela and intrigued by the money that my family had."

"He sounds an extraordinary man."

"More so in those days. It wasn't unusual for him to come back with other women and expect me to participate in his sexual fantasies. I thank God that he was never interested in men because I would have had to have drawn the line."

"But you let him move his mistress in downstairs. Didn't that bother you?"

"My husband has not aged well. His beautiful blonde hair has gone, and he is semi-bald. His stomach now bulges over his trousers, and his face is lined and battered by stress through his work. Marina Ferro was a beautiful creature and did him good. He was happy, and a happy Fabio makes people's lives better, including my own. Am I shocking you, inspector?"

"So, what you are telling me is that for you there is no problem with him having other women. Does that mean you can have other men?"

"After Fabio, I don't want any other men. It's just sex, inspector. All that Fabio wanted off Marina Ferro was half an hour of pleasure. Marriage is a lot more than this. He shared his soul with me, and that is worth so much more than a couple of orgasms and a quick goodbye."

"Do you love your husband?"

"Of course. And he loves me."

"Did he love Marina Ferro?"

"No."

"How can you be so sure?"

"Because I know Fabio. He loved her body, as would any sane man."

"Did you know that she was seeing somebody else?"

"I didn't, but it doesn't surprise me. Fabio wanted more than his body could give him. He has arthritis in his neck and shoulders so is not very active. These days he usually just lies there and lets the woman do the work. Including me." She laughed at the look of shock on Visco's face. "Yes, inspector, we still have a physical relationship. I have certain needs as well."

Visco changed the subject. "So how long did you say you've been married?"

"Twenty years."

"When did he ask you to marry him?"

"From the look on your face, inspector I think what you meant to say was why. You are a gentleman. I can respect that in a man. He used me to further his career. Or rather, he used my money and my father's connections. Fabio is a one-man mafia, but everyone loves him. I'm not delusional. If it had been my friend Angela who had the money, he would have chosen her. He was at the age when he needed a front of respectability to get into the higher echelons of political power. As a single man, he was too much of a loose cannon.

Married, he was just like the rest. They all have wives and lovers. The only difference with Fabio is that he had ten times more affairs. It was like being part of a harem. Do you think that Muslim wives get jealous of each other?"

"I'm not sure. Probably not, but you're not Muslim."

"Yes, but my husband can't be cured. You either have to put up with it or walk away. Where would I go? I prefer my life here."

Where indeed thought Visco. He instinctively felt that he was in the presence of somebody that was very honest. He wondered, though, if she was being honest with herself. She wasn't particularly beautiful in the conventional sense of the word, but she did have a certain something that made you look twice. Visco liked her and felt relaxed in her company, which was strange for him. "Did Marina Ferro know that you knew about her?"

"I have no idea."

"Why do you think she put up with living so close to you? She must have known that his wife was only a few floors above her."

"I think money and a certain amount of security played its part."

"But what would have happened when your husband got bored with this woman. Would he have thrown her out onto the streets?"

"Fabio is not like that, but I don't know what he would have done. Knowing him, he would have probably paid her off and installed somebody else."

"Did he see her the night she was murdered?"

"No, he arrived back after midnight and came straight home."

"How can you be so sure?"

"Because I was waiting up, and heard the lift."

"And?"

"From the terrace, I saw his car arriving. If he goes to see her, he always walks up the stairs. I counted the floors. He came straight from the ground to the top."

"So he didn't see her every day."

"No. He only went down when he had the urge for sex. I don't think he would have gone and engaged in small talk. That wasn't what the arrangement was all about."

"What did you do on the evening of the murder?"

"My mother came around, and we watched TV together. We both fell asleep watching some game show. She woke me up just before the news at eleven, said she was tired and left."

"So she doesn't live in the building."

"No. She lives near San Antonio. She gets bored being stuck in the house with my dad, so she often comes to keep me company."

"Does your mother know about the arrangement with Ferro?"

"I never told her. She and my husband don't get on that well, but only because she thinks he leaves me on my own too much. My mother and father are not the sort of people that would understand his promiscuity. I would be too embarrassed to talk about it with them. They are devout Catholics and do a lot with the Church. " She looked at her watch. " I have an appointment with my mother now, and I don't want to keep her waiting. Do you have any further questions?"

"Not at the moment, Mrs. Conti. I know where you live, so I will come and see you again I'm sure. I also need to speak to your husband."

"When you do talk to him, please don't tell him about my frankness about his sexual problems. I told you so you would understand."

"I can't promise that. This is a murder inquiry, and as such, I will do anything necessary to find the killer."

"I understand, inspector."

She stood up and held out her hand. It was a very masculine gesture, and Visco could see that although she looked soft on the outside, she had a core of steel. "I'm home most of the time, inspector, if you need to speak to me again."

She went out and closed the door behind her. Visco sniffed the air. Her perfume was expensive and had a hint of vanilla. He couldn't deny that he was impressed with Ana Conti but disgusted by the antics of her husband. He smiled as he let himself out. It must have been the influence of the Catholic Church and his catechism lessons that made him turn out this way. That priest had a lot to answer for.

CHAPTER SIX

Visco thought about Marina Ferro as he drove back to the police HQ. During his long career, he had known lots of women who were almost exactly the same as her. They were, more often than not, born into poverty and used the only asset that they had to try and climb out.

If they lived to reach old age, they became hard and bitter. They saw life through cynical eyes and realized that they had wasted theirs. Others, got into drink and drugs to anesthetize the pain, while girls like Marina, wound up dead.

He imagined her early life on the streets of Rome. Standing on dark street corners waiting for cars to arrive. Money changing hands before she led them up stairs to a bedroom in some run-down rooming house. It must have been a step up for her when she started to visit rich Arabs and Americans, and meeting Fabio Conti must have made her believe that her troubles were over. In fact, they were just beginning.

Luca was working behind his desk when he arrived back. As always in summer, the heat inside the building was oppressive, and the ceiling fans did nothing other than shift the hot air around and make papers fly off tables. He wished for cooler temperatures but realized that it would get worse before it got better. By the time August arrived, most people would be wishing the weather had stayed like this.

"Anything happened since I was away?"

Luca glanced up from his paperwork. "We have set up the usual road blocks, and I have put men to watch the hotel and the nightclub. He is going to turn up somewhere, and all of our men on the street have been issued with his photograph. It hasn't been put out on the news yet, as we don't want him to go to ground."

"Let's give it until tomorrow. If we still haven't made contact, we can see if a photo in the local press and on TV will bring forward some members of the public."

"Oh, and the doctor phoned and asked if you would phone him when you had a minute."

Visco picked up the telephone and dialed. After only a couple of rings, the police pathologist came on the line.

"I have done the post-mortem. Death was caused by the knife wound to the throat. The knife was big. I would say that the blade had serrated edges. My guess is that it was a kitchen knife used for cutting up meat. There wasn't one found in the apartment, I believe."

"She was knifed from the front?"

"Yes, the entry hole is typical of a thrust by somebody standing in front. It is a pretty nasty way to kill. Either by a professional killer with no feelings either way or somebody that loathed and detested this woman."

"A professional would have used a proper knife or even a gun with a silencer. If it is true about the kitchen knife, we are looking for somebody who hated Marina Ferro. Would you say it was a man or a woman, doctor?"

"You tell me. It was a person who was roughly the same size as the victim. I can tell that by the angle of entry. To deliver this type of knife wound didn't take a lot of strength, but the power behind the thrust must have been generated by a lot of anger. I wonder if there had been an argument before."

"Was death instantaneous?"

"Fairly, though still not pleasant. The stomach had undigested food. Pasta, tomato and red wine."

"Anything else?"

"Hardly, but I will send you a full written report tomorrow. I asked you to telephone because I assumed you needed as much information on the murder as possible."

Visco hung up and headed for the door. "If anything else happens today, you can get me at home." He was tired and saw no reason to be in the office.

He drove home, and his wife opened the door before he had a chance to turn the handle. She didn't scold him for being over two hours late but handed him a chilled glass of wine and a fresh shirt.

"Your meal is ready. Are you in for the rest of the day?" She knew, of course, that he wasn't. She was a bit of a detective herself and realized that even though he had gingerly changed into a fresh cotton shirt. He had not removed his shoes. A police inspector's life was never routine, but Visco had a certain predictability, which made him a creature of habit.

After eating and listening patiently to his wife discussing her day, he poured himself a second glass of wine and a shot of grappa. He poured his coffee and drank it standing up.

"Do you think you will be long?" Said his wife

"A couple of hours."

"Well don't do too much, remember, you are not getting any younger, and you need your sleep."

Visco kissed his wife on the cheek and walked out to his car. After the cool air-conditioned atmosphere of his living room, the heat took his breath away, and he was instantly sweating. He had to wait another five minutes before the big Alfa's cooling system kicked in and he felt human again.

On the street where the Blue Anchor was situated, there was a definite change of atmosphere as the night wore on. When Visco arrived, the obscure figures were already emerging from the shadows and plying their trade. It was evident what most of the women were up to and what they were waiting for. What was less easy to define was the reasons why a lot of the men were there. Some were seeking cheap sex; others were selling drugs and a few, keeping an eye on their women. These were the pimps, the ones that Visco despised the most. They made their living out of misery, and preyed on the weak and vulnerable, then tossed them aside.

There were no winners on this street, just people in various states of unhappiness and desperation. He didn't include himself on this list. How could he? He was on the side of the good and zealous. He was probably the most desperate of all of the people gathered here tonight. Somebody who wanted to save people from themselves. A thankless task that could never be achieved. As always, Visco was an optimist. If he weren't, then the job would have driven him mad, years ago. He contented himself with laughing at the men who had just come to watch. These were the sex tourists who were too shy to do it but got their kicks with their fantasies about women degrading themselves for a couple of lire.

The neon sign of the Blue Anchor, curiously, burned crimson. It shone its light like a pool on the pavement in front of the main door. As he approached, he could hear muted music from inside. It was the usual blend of trashy Euro Pop that he despised so much. He noted the presence of a plain-clothes police officer, with a slight nod of his head, and pushed his way inside.

No sooner had he gone through the velvet curtain that led him into the main room, than several customers beat a hasty exit. As he walked over to the bar, heads were turning away in the hope that he wouldn't recognize them. Visco was well known all over the Gulf of Policastro and was not good for business. The owner came towards him and didn't look happy.

"I thought that I told your monkey that we hadn't seen Barone. We are not expecting him in tonight."

"My monkey was not convinced and is too polite to make a nuisance of himself. Unfortunately, for you, I'm not that polite. I thought that maybe a visit from me might help your business." He looked around as more people headed towards the door. The owner took his arm and steered him over to a booth in the corner. There was a sign on the table that said reserved.

"Sit down here, inspector. What can I get you to drink? On the house, of course."

Visco expected nothing less. It was part of the perks of his job.

"Get me a Peroni with a large grappa."

The owner clicked his fingers, and a waiter appeared. "A Peroni and a large glass of grappa for the inspector." He turned his attention to Visco. "So is it me that you want to talk to?"

Visco shook his head. "You know that Barone is a pimp. Shit usually sticks together at the bottom of a sewer. Who's in tonight that he is friends with?"

"His best friend is Francesco Masotti. He's the one sitting by the bar with the white suit, sunglasses and greased back hair."

"Are you sure you are not lying to me. I rather like this booth. Maybe I will come here every night. That should do your trade a power of good." As if to emphasize what Visco was saying, several girls who had been on the dance floor, picked up their handbags and headed for the door."

"He's the one that you need to talk to. I'll send him over. Then will you leave?"

"That depends."

"On what?"

"Depends on how much useful information I get, and how vindictive I feel. At the moment, I am feeling in a nasty mood. I could be having a peaceful evening at home listening to Mozart, instead of talking to scum like you and listening to music like this. Send him over, and make that order two beers and two doubles. Now run along, there's a good fellow."

While he was waiting, Visco studied the room. There was a mixture of Southern Italian society that included early season tourists and locals. There were a certain number of prostitutes, but they didn't seem to be too bothered about picking up clients. Maybe they were waiting for him to leave before returning to their business. What was so typical of the area was that mixed with the low-class street girls were shop girls, secretaries, and students. Nobody moralized here, though they remained in their own groups and rarely acknowledged each other. Most of the females were here to dance and the men to watch and make their moves as the night wore on. For the good-looking males, there was always a hint of getting their sex for free, while the older men knew that they would need to bargain cleverly for it.

The man in the white suit and sunglasses came over and slid into the vacant space behind the table.

"What do you want to drink?" Asked Visco.

"Nothing off you. I'm particular who I drink with."

Visco ignored the remark. "So you are Francesco Masotti, is this correct?"

The man nodded and stared idly into space. Without prompting, he said. "You are making a huge mistake going after Dario Barone. He loved Marina and would never have done her any harm."

"So why doesn't he come and speak to us?"

"Maybe it's because you have already made up your minds. It's always the same with police. They want to do as little work as possible. Why don't you go and find out who the real killer is and stop chasing Dario? He is upset enough at losing his girlfriend."

"So how well do you know Barone?"

"Better than most."

"So where is he now?"

"This, I don't know."

"You do know that he was arrested for pimping girls, don't you?"

"And that makes him a killer, does it?"

"No, but it doesn't help his reputation as being honest. Did he meet Marina when she was a call girl in Rome?"

"How the hell do I know?"

"Well, I think that he did and that he let her carry on making money as a prostitute and was living off immoral earnings. In my opinion, pimps are the lowest of the low, Francesco. They make money off young girls and drain the life out of them. Isn't that what you do?"

"You can't say that."

"I can say what I like." In a fraction of a second, a flash of cold steel whirled through the air; Francesco felt the handcuff tighten over his wrist. He instinctively tried to rise from the seat, but Visco tugged him back down and whispered in his ear. "You are under arrest, Mr. Masotti. I will take you down to the station now, unless..."

"Unless what?"

"Unless you give me some information that can help me find Barone. You would be doing him a favor, and helping yourself out of a huge problem."

"I haven't got any problems."

"Give me a couple of minutes to think, and I'm sure I can come up with a list that will put you in the penitentiary for at least a couple of years. Maybe you killed Marina Ferro. People can be bought to say anything, or didn't you know this."

"You can't do this?"

"Watch me. Are you so naive? You said yourself that I am looking for somebody to blame for the murder. If it's not Barone, then you will do. You fancied Marina and wanted her for yourself. She rejected you and your pride couldn't take it. Of course, I have several witnesses who saw you come out of the apartment with blood on your shirt. Oh yes, I almost forgot. We found the murder weapon in you flat. That was your biggest mistake, Masotti. It is funny how a murderer always leaves at least one clue."

"That's corrupt."

"It's the way of the world these days. We are all at it, politicians, pimps, police inspectors! You can never find an honest cop when you want one, and I believe that at this moment in time, you really do want one."

"You bastard. Ok, what do you want to know?"

CHAPTER SEVEN

The gravel in the driveway crackled under the tires of Visco's Alpha. He looked at his watch and sighed. It was after two o'clock, and he wished he was in bed with his wife and a good book. One of his officers stepped out of the shadows as he approached the small beach house on the coast road that if you traveled on it long enough would end up in Sicily.

"The villa looks empty, sir and there is no sign of Barone."

Things had moved fast since Francesco Masotti had given Visco this address. He claimed Barone rented it and that he was hiding there because he was scared of the police. Visco could understand this mentality, knowing as he did the amount of corruption that there was with his fellow officers on the force. It wasn't that his colleagues were bad people. It was just that they weren't paid very well and the criminals could afford to pay them more. That's why the large mafia families were untouchable. In the south, the corruption ran from the top, right down to the lowliest police officer on traffic control. It had always been that way, and you needed to accept it or find another job. That other job, whatever it was, looked very promising to the inspector at that moment. He rubbed his eyes, took out his gun from the glove compartment and slid it under his belt.

He looked at the front of the villa with a cold professional eye. "So this is where he is hiding? Have you looked inside?"

"Not yet, sir, but we have road blocks on all of the major routes, and my partner is around the back of the building."

Visco cut him short. "How about moving my car out of sight, while I have a look around."

Visco walked up the road towards a small wood; he kept in the shadows, found a spot and waited. After about twenty minutes, a large Fiat approached the villa, dropped a man off and drove away at speed. The figure was caught in the thin light of one of the police officer's torch. It was definitely Dario Barone. He must have been shocked, but he recovered quickly. He punched the policeman and ran back up the road to where Visco was waiting. By the time he reached the inspector, he was out of breath. Visco stepped out from behind a tree and trained his gun on the running man. The sight of the weapon stopped him.

"I believe that you are under arrest, Mr. Barone. Do you want to come quietly, or do I have to put a hole in one of your kneecaps?"

The man raised his hands slowly.

Visco moved behind him and kicked his legs away. Barone fell heavily to the ground and grunted in pain as his nose hit the hard tarmac and exploded blood down his chin. Visco grabbed his arms, handcuffed him and searched his clothes expertly for a concealed weapon. There was none. By the time the two police officers arrived, it was all over.

"Take him to the station. I'll be there in the morning to interview him. Right now, I'm going home to catch up on some sleep." As he was walking away, he shouted over his shoulder. "Oh yes, and can you get a team into the house and tear it apart. We are particularly looking for the murder weapon."

Barone's face was pale, and there were dark lines under his eyes from lack of sleep. He was sitting behind a plain green desk in one of two interview rooms at the police HQ in Scalea. He looked like a trapped animal, and this was how Visco wanted him to be. He could have traveled back and interviewed him straight away, but the inspector was a wily old fox. He needed the sleep, and Barone needed time alone in a police cell to realize that this was what he was facing for the rest of this life.

Even though it was against the rules, he told the policewoman by the door to leave. "Now there is only you and me in the room, Barone, so we can speak more openly. I can get to know you better. Do you want a drink? Have you had some coffee this morning?" He went over to a table at the back of the room and poured out two coffees from a flask. He handed him a cup and took a sip himself. It was bitter, as it always was in this room.

"I think that we both know that you are in serious trouble."

"Why?" Barone's voice was hoarse, like a man who had gone days without food, drink or sleep and had been smoking heavily. The inspector noticed how nicotine stained his hands were. He was unshaven and his hair disheveled and in need of washing.

"Have you eaten?"

"What is it with you? No, I've not eaten, but you sound like my mother. Just get on with it and fit me up for a murder I didn't commit. Maybe, you can throw in other things that I haven't done, like a couple of burglaries. Let's face it, your mind is made up about me, and nothing I say is going to change it."

He seemed to be younger than his age, and the ranting was just nerves. Visco felt sorry for him. Even in the warmth of another gloriously warm day, he was trembling from head to toe.

"I don't think that you did it."

"What?"

"If you did it, why did you phone her up the next day? Are you that brilliant? Was it a ploy to make us think that you didn't know? I wasn't convinced before, but looking at you I am certain."

"Certain of what?"

"Certain you haven't got the brains or the bottle, son."

Barone burst into tears. It must have been the first time that he had let himself go since the death of his girlfriend. He was crying like a baby and hiding his face with both hands. Visco didn't interrupt. He guessed that Barone had been more concerned about the implication that he had killed Marina, rather than the death itself. Being face to face with his accuser had brought out all of the emotion that he had bottled up.

"I swear to God that I didn't kill her, inspector."

Visco believed him. He had seen too many guilty men and women in this room not to know the difference between the truth and lies. Even though he knew that Barone was a pimp that preyed on young girls he looked more like an office clerk than someone who was capable of such despicable things.

He repeated again, "I didn't kill her."

"Calm down, son. I believe you. I wasn't lying when I said that you didn't have the bottle. You may have some bad morals, but I don't see you as a killer."

Barone reached into his pocket and brought out a packet of cigarettes. He lit one with a hand that was still shaking.

"You did see her on the evening she was murdered, didn't you?"

"I did, but only for a few minutes. We argued, and I left."

"What did you argue about?"

"Something and nothing. She was in a bad mood, and as always wanted to take it out on me. I rang her up the next day to see if she was still depressed."

"So why do you think she was depressed."

"She had made up her mind to leave the apartment and get out from under Conti's clutches. She was in two minds."

"In what way?"

"Marina and I shared the same sort of background. She was dragged up with no money. In the apartment she had security and money but hated the feeling of being controlled. She wanted out but knew that it would mean she didn't have security or money anymore."

"So she was leaving one person who controlled her for another."

"What? You think I controlled Marina? You have to be kidding."

"Weren't you her pimp?"

"Marina used the best asset that she had. Her body was what men craved for, and she knew that if she used it, she could earn good money. I was never her pimp. I used to protect her if she needed it, but most of the time she could protect herself. You have got the wrong idea entirely about her. She was a tough cookie, not a dainty wallflower."

"Do you think that she loved you?"

"I think she did."

"So how did you feel about her relationship with Fabio Conti?"

"Marina was her own woman. If you tried to direct her in any way, she would go in the opposite direction."

"Yet, she let Conti control her."

"To some degree, but Marina had power over men when it came to sex."

"How?"

"She was good. Very good. A woman that good can get whatever she wants. She told me that Conti could hardly do it. He could barely manage anything. Having her was just for his ego."

Visco watched Barone's face very carefully before he asked his next question. "Are you sure she was not making that up so as to not hurt your feelings. Maybe they were having great sex together."

Barone shrugged and shook his head. "Marina was a lot of things, but she would never lie to spare anybody's feelings. She told you how it was and you had to accept or leave."

"And you didn't leave."

"Once you have tasted caviar, you are not going to go back to eating squid."

"She was that good?"

"The best."

"Who killed her?"

I have been racking my brain and keep coming back to Conti. Maybe she told him that she was leaving and he couldn't take it."

Visco had to admit that this was a theory he had thought about himself.

"Where did you meet her?"

"We met in Rome. She was working hotels in the center and didn't have a protector; that's dangerous. She offered me ten percent, and I took it."

"And here in Maratea?"

"She disappeared from Rome, and I didn't hear from her for months. She phoned me up out of the blue and told me she was in an apartment being paid for by somebody very rich. She said she was bored and would I like to come down."

"And you did."

"Believe me, inspector. She had that sort of power, and besides, I missed her and Rome was dead. I needed a change of air."

"So you moved to the area just because Marina Ferro asked."

"Moved back to the area. I'm originally from Scalea, and I have relatives near here."

"So tell me about her friends."

"Marina didn't have any friends. She didn't need them; she was too busy trying to survive."

"Surely she had people that she would talk to, even if they weren't friends."

"Believe it or not, she was a hooker with a heart. Ask Hugo Berlinski."

"Her cleaner?"

"That's the one. She talked to him a lot and gave him extra money to help him out. That was the kind of woman she was. If you needed help, she would give you what you needed. It's funny that she wasn't very good at sorting her own life out."

"So what was her relationship with Berlinski?"

"Not what you are implying, inspector. Conti must have found him for her, and she got talking and felt sorry for him. I guess they talked because, for her, he didn't represent a threat."

"Anybody else that you can think of?"

"No. All her family is dead, and she didn't have any old school friends if that's what you mean. She barely made it through middle school. She hated the man on the door. That bastard Pardo was being paid by Conti to keep an eye on her. I had to wait until he finished his shift for the night before I visited. Even then, he sometimes saw me leaving in the morning if I happened to sleep late."

"That sounds like the actions of a jealous man."

"It's the actions of a prat. Marina was his property, and he wanted to make sure that she stayed that way. Until he didn't need her anymore."

"So are you saying that he might have been trying to get rid of her?"

"I don't think so. She was stunning. Girls like Marina take some finding. He must have thought it was his birthdays all rolled into one when she agreed to take the apartment."

"Did you love her?"

"Yes."

"You knew her before she ever became involved with Conti, yet you let her sleep with other men for money."

"That was different. Like I said before, you couldn't stop her doing anything."

"Were you taking advantage of Conti's money?"

"How do you mean?"

"I mean, was she giving you anything?"

"A couple of gifts, nothing more."

"So you never took advantage of Conti's wealth?"

He shook his head and lit another cigarette. Visco noticed that his hands had stopped shaking.

"If she had left him, what would you have done?"

"We would have lived together."

"Like in Rome? Would you have used her body to bring money in?"

"It's the only thing that either of us knew. We would have probably gone back to Rome."

Visco got up and moved towards the door. "You're free to go, Mr. Barone. But don't leave the area.

CHAPTER EIGHT

Visco drove to the address he had been given for Hugo Berlinski in Lower Maratea. The building he parked in front of was clearly in need of repair and looked like it hadn't received a coat of paint since it was built. The noise of children playing in the corridors and balconies of the condominium was oppressive, and he wondered how many families were crammed into the four floors.

Berlinski's apartment was on the first floor, which was lucky, considering that the lift was out of order. The stairs were steep and chipped. The building was full of unpleasant smells, cracked walls, and rotting rubbish. The fact that it overlooked a cliff did not go unnoticed by the inspector.

"I'm not in," shouted a voice when he knocked the door of number three.

Visco tried the handle, and the door opened. Berlinski was sitting on the settee watching TV. He didn't look surprised to see Visco but didn't acknowledge his presence either. He simply waited for him the say something.

"I need to ask you a few questions."

"Ask away." He changed the channel and then switched the TV off in disgust.

"When I talked to you at the apartment of Marina Ferro, you didn't tell me that you were friendly with her and that you often chatted."

"You didn't ask me."

"Well, I'm asking you now, sir."

"We did occasionally talk, but not about anything serious."

"She also gave you money."

"You must have been talking to her boyfriend. He was a jealous bastard. Maybe you should be talking to him about the murder, rather than pestering innocent people like me."

"You are telling me that you think Dario Barone killed Marina?"

"That would be doing your job for you, inspector. Why would I want to do that? Like I told you before, the only thing that I know is that I didn't kill her."

"Get your hat and coat, Berlinski. I want to take you in so that I can interview you in conditions that are more formal. This may take a couple of days. I'm not arresting you, yet."

"You can't do that."

"I can do what I want. I am also going to look into where you came from and why you are here. Are you sure that you are not Russian? How do we know you are who you say you are? This is all going to take some time, so pack an overnight bag."

"OK, I get it. What do you want to know?"

"Did you know that Fabio Conti was paying for the apartment?"

"He hired me to clean. I suspected that he was using her, but she never said anything to me. She talked more about her boyfriend."

"Dario Barone?"

"That's him."

"What did she tell you?"

"She said that they were thinking of going back to Rome together. She asked me what I thought. I told her that she didn't fit in the building. It was full of rich old snobs that looked down on her. She needed a big city like Rome to come alive again."

"What would you say was her state of mind before she was killed?"

"Happy. She often went through phases of depression when she complained to me about her life. The day before she was killed, we drank coffee on the balcony, and she said that she was going to look for a new house either in Rome or Milan. She asked me, which I thought would be better."

"Did she ever mention Conti?"

"Not by name. She did say that her life was more complicated than it looked. She told me that one of the reasons she wanted to get away, was because she didn't like to feel under pressure."

"What did she mean by that?"

"The way I saw it, inspector, she was implying that there was somebody else besides Dario Barone. This someone would not be very happy if she tried to leave. In my humble opinion, I think she was planning to disappear because she was scared."

"Scared of Fabio Conti?"

"I guess so."

"Do you think that she was in love with Dario Barone?"

"For sure."

"Did she have a lot of money off Conti?"

"She always had money and was very generous. She never told me where she got it from and why should I ask."

"Do you think that she was also very generous with her boyfriend?"

"Marina Ferro was a beautiful lady in every sense. She was generous with everybody except herself. Do you have any more questions, inspector? I have another job to go to."

"More cleaning work?"

"No, I have a job in a bakery shop. It is better hours and more money than cleaning."

"Are you sure that you didn't see a murder weapon?"

"Positive."

"You do know that interfering with a crime scene is a criminal offense, don't you?"

"Why would I do something like this?"

"Why indeed. You would be particularly stupid if you did because we would find out. We always find out things like that. If I do, then I will be back."

"Is that a threat, inspector?"

"That is more of a promise. So be very careful." With that, he went back down to his car and drove the short distance to his office.

CHAPTER NINE

Fabiana Volsi watched through the window as Visco got out of his car in front of her shop. She looked a lot younger than her fifty years and was dressed elegantly in the mode of most, typically, middle-class Italians.

Visco entered the dress shop, and a bell above the door announced his presence to the empty room. The shop was dimly lit and as silent as the grave. The dresses that hung from rails looked like they were expensive and he wondered how the owner could compete with the cheap Chinese shop next door. He concluded that she couldn't and was more than likely kept afloat by a rich husband.

He spotted Ana Conti's mother, Fabiana, as soon as he entered and for a second, thought it was the daughter. They looked so alike and the mother so young.

"Inspector Visco. I have been expecting you, though I naturally assumed you would visit me at home."

"You recognize me?"

"From your picture in the newspaper. You are something of a celebrity among the police in this area. You have had an illustrious career."

"Helped by the stupidity of the criminals, I think."

She laughed. "You are hard on yourself. I like that in a man."

Visco wondered what else she liked in a man. Everything about her was sexual. The innuendo in her voice and the way she looked at him and moved her body. In this, her daughter must have taken after her father. She invited him to come into the back room of the shop and indicated for him to sit down on a leather settee. She crammed herself in next to him, and he could feel the heat coming off her.

Up close, he realized that she was slightly taller and slimmer than her daughter. Her skin was pure white as if she very rarely went outside.

"I assume that you have come to ask me questions about the death of Fabio's lover."

"You assume correctly. You daughter gave us this address. She said that you were there on the night of the murder. Is that correct?"

"Yes, I left around eleven."

"Your daughter said that she hadn't told you about her husband's lover. How come you know?"

"She told me last night, but we all knew what Fabio is like."

"How come?"

"Most women know instinctively if a man is a womanizer. It's in the eyes and the way that he talks to you. For instance, inspector. You are a family man; you love your wife and wouldn't dream of ever being unfaithful. You have honest eyes."

"You make me sound very boring."

"It's what most women crave for. An honest man. It's not in the Italian male's persona. In the south especially, to be a ragamuffin womanizer is something to cherish."

"I take it you don't like your son in law."

"I loathe him, but don't tell Ana. She has wasted her life on him, but what can a mother do. Children will never listen. If you push one way, they will go another. Even her father doesn't like Fabio, and he loves everybody. Do you have children, inspector?"

"Two girls in university. One studying law and the other, medicine."

"So you have lived with three women. No wonder you like your job so much. It keeps you out of the way when the hormones start flying."

Visco had never thought about it like that. She was leading him off track. "Do you visit your daughter very often?"

"Yes, she gets lonely. She is like a prisoner in that awful apartment.

"Did she invite you over the night of the murder?"

"More or less. She asked me what I was doing, and I said I wasn't doing that much."

"So what did you do that night?"

"I cooked for her, and then we watched TV. I left around eleven."

"Was there somebody on the reception desk?"

"Pardo? You have to be joking. He has his coat on waiting to leave as soon as it gets dark. I often wonder why nobody reports him. Probably because he knows too much about the comings and goings."

"You say that your daughter never talked about her husband having a live-in-lover. Do you think that is normal?"

"She doesn't tell me everything about her life, and I don't tell her everything about mine. Knowing my daughter, I would have been surprised if she had told me."

"Do you think it bothered her?"

"I'm her mother, not her intimate friend. You should ask her. One thing I can vouch for is that she is always brutally honest. So when are you going to arrest him?"

"Arrest who?"

"Fabio. Isn't it obvious that he killed her?"

"Not to me. Why is it so obvious to you?"

"Who else could it be?"

"Who indeed? That's what I intend to find out." Visco got up and made his way out. "I know where to find you if I need to ask you any more questions. In the meantime, if you can think of anything that's relevant, give me a call." He tossed a card onto the desk and headed for the street. Outside, after the comparative coolness of the air-conditioned shop, it was like stepping into a furnace. He was once again instantly sweating. By the time he had walked to his car, his shirt was saturated. He made a mental note to talk to his boss about installing a shower in his office for days like these.

CHAPTER TEN

Visco arrived at the Town Hall in Maratea with the intention of finally interviewing Fabio Conti. He was given the news that Conti and his assistant had left for Rome and wouldn't be back until the evening. He wasn't expecting this but made the best of his bad luck by visiting Conti's department, which was situated on the second floor.

He found the office fuller than he had expected, with secretaries and assistants either engaged in telephoning or typing. He chose an older woman who looked less busy. She had gray hair and a mole on her chin.

"Who is in charge here?" Visco passed his ID in front of her face, and she visibly stiffened.

"I'm Mr. Conti's personal secretary. He is not in at the moment."

"That's OK. I would like to talk to you. Is there somewhere private that we can go?"

She hesitated and then beckoned him to follow her through a door at the far end of the room. The door had Fabio Conti's name on it, and Visco knew that the space behind it wasn't going to be small and cramped. He wasn't let down. The room that they entered was huge. Behind an expensive mahogany desk, there was a window that stretched the whole length of one wall. It gave a panoramic view of the bay in all of its splendor.

He noticed that there was another exit. "Where does that door lead to?"

"It's a fire exit and leads to Mr. Conti's private car park."

Visco sat down in front of the desk and waited for the gray haired lady to take a seat. She wasn't confident enough to sit on her boss's leather chair but chose a wooden hard backed one next to him.

"I want you to tell me about the events last Thursday. Where you at work during the day?"

She nodded. "We had a TV crew down from Rome, and there was a meeting that started at nine o'clock in the evening. I was there and took the minutes."

"And was Fabio Conti there?"

"Yes. He was the chairman."

"Can you tell me a little about what happened that day? For example, what time did he arrive?"

"Mr. Conti always comes into the office about eight. That is if he is not in Rome, representing the region, or on TV."

"Yes, of course, I almost forgot," lied Visco. "Mr. Conti has his own talk show on TV. How does that work?"

"Mr. Conti has a chat show, which goes out on the weekends. He is usually away in Rome on a Monday. He records the show, and then stays the night." She added, "He has a house in Rome."

"Very nice, I envy him. Can you explain what the meeting was about, and Mr. Conti's movements beforehand?"

"The meeting was about lowering taxation for people with agricultural land that produces vegetables and fruit for the sole consumption of the family."

"How many people were present?"

"At least two hundred. It's a popular gripe at the moment."

"So the meeting started at nine. What time did it finish?"

"Eleven."

"Did Mr. Conti go straight home?"

"No, he talked to a few people then went to his office about eleven. He told me to go home at this time, so I don't know what time he went home."

"So he was alone from this time."

"His assistant could still have been here. I couldn't say for sure, though."

"And his assistant is?"

"Angela Amuso. She helps him with all aspects of his job, but particularly the media work. She has been with him for many years."

Visco wrote the name down in his notebook. "So does he usually leave the office by going through the typing pool or use his personal stairs?"

"Most of the time he would come through and say goodnight to the staff. That's the kind of person he is. I would imagine that he would have done the same that night, though of course there would have been nobody around."

"Not even a doorman on the main door?"

"No, not at that time of night. He would have let himself out with a key."

"So you don't know anything about his whereabouts after eleven thirty. Am I correct?"

"Yes but..."

Visco got up and walked to the door. Thank you, Mrs..."

"That's Miss. My name is Paula; I'm not married."

As he made his way to the car park, he wondered how many of the women in his department could be involved sexually with their boss. He discounted Paula as being too plain looking but reckoned that she would not have said no to the idea.

CHAPTER ELEVEN

At nine o'clock that evening, Visco's Alpha was discreetly parked outside the building were Fabio Conti lived. It was growing dark, and there was a delightful breeze coming in from the harbor. There was a dim light glowing in the reception, but the rest of the building was in darkness, except for the top floor. He assumed that this was where Ana Conti was preparing dinner and awaiting her husband's return from Rome.

The nature of the building meant that at any one time most of the apartments were unoccupied. It was probably at its fullest when August arrived, and Italy shut down for the month. This was the time when anybody with even the tiniest space to rent, could make a fortune, as all of Italy was on holiday.

He had been waiting an hour and was not in a good mood. He had been like this ever since he had left the town hall. He hated dealing with pompous political figures and wondered what influence Conti would have with his superiors. Lean too hard on the wrong person, and you could find yourself on traffic duty no matter how big your reputation was.

His mood had not been enhanced by the report handed to him by his assistant Luca. This was on the tenants of the condominium. It was a three-page ramble that told him nothing, except that nobody had heard or seen anything out of the normal. Visco had worked on a couple of other cases that still hadn't been solved, and made a few unimportant telephone calls just to pass the time. On a whim, he decided to go and wait for the arrival of Conti.

At ten 'clock a silver Mercedes pulled up, and Conti got out of the passenger side. He stood motionless for a while on the pavement and was obviously deep in conversation with the driver. This was a woman who must have been his assistant. His features were picked out by a streetlight. He was tall and broad shouldered, but even from the distance he was watching from, Visco noticed the bulging stomach over the belt of his trousers and the thinning jet-black hair that was so obviously dyed. He was dressed in beige Chinos and a short sleeve shirt and tie. He gave the impression of a man staring impatiently at old age and trying his very best to ignore it. His stooping shoulders and humorless face were typical of the political class in the south. There was a certain arrogance that was subtly on display, which Visco was always aware of with these types. He wouldn't have got to the position of power that he was in without having it, and it came from a natural contempt for anything that couldn't be used or purchased to further a career.

The woman behind the wheel was doing most of the talking. She was more than likely telling him about his appointments for the next day. She eventually got out of the car and walked with him to the entrance. She had a brief case in her hand, which looked heavy. She handed it to him at the door, walked back to her car and drove off. Visco followed.

After a journey into the mountains that lasted about fifteen minutes, she turned into the drive of a whitewashed villa, parked and got out. She was stumpy with short gray hair and a plain face. She turned as the Alpha drove through the gates, and Visco got out.

"Angela Amuso?"

"Yes." She didn't look frightened or surprised and waited for Visco to come up close.

"My name is Inspector Visco, and I would like to ask you a few questions about the murder of Marina Ferro."

She turned and spoke as she was walking towards the front door. "You had better come in, Inspector."

The villa was small but spotlessly clean. She showed him into a scarcely furnished living room that was dominated by a huge television. He noticed that one of the paintings on the wall was a watercolor of Fabio Conti when he was at the height of his sexual prowess.

Angela Amuso was not pretty to look at, so he assumed that she must have other qualities to have risen so high. He suspected that these qualities had a lot to do with organization. Even this room with its coordinated bookcase and furniture and show house blandness, looked as if it had been organized by somebody fanatical about order and symmetry.

She beckoned him to sit down in an armchair, and she chose the settee. She waited patiently and stared with dark brown unblinking eyes into his. She had a certain power that went beyond look, and Visco now understood how she got her job.

"How long have you worked for Fabio Conti?"

"About ten years."

"What type of things do you do for him?"

"You name it; I do it. I organize his working life, and clear up all of his little problems."

"Does he get a lot of problems?"

"More than most. It comes with his position of power. You need to stay active to keep on top of the heap. Somebody is always ready to take your place."

"Would you say that you have a good relationship with your boss?"

"Yes."

"Were you with him on the night of the murder of Marina Ferro?"

"I dropped him off as usual in front of his building."

"Did he seem normal?"

"Yes."

"And did you see him during the evening of the taxation meeting?"

"I didn't go to the meeting. I was in my office doing work. He telephoned me just before midnight to take him home. I waited in the car park for him."

"How long does it take to get from the town hall to his apartment?"

"About ten minutes at that time of night because there is no traffic."

Visco knew that this was correct because he had timed it himself. "So he was in full view of everyone until about eleven. There was a period of fifty minutes when he was on his own. He could have made the trip."

"He didn't have a car."

"If you use the short cut, and climb the steps into the old town, you can walk from the town hall to his apartment in around fifteen minutes. You could do it in ten if you jogged."

"I will have to take your word for it."

Visco knew that this was correct as he had run and walked the distance earlier that evening."

"Would you say that your boss was a fit man?"

"He doesn't work out if that is what you mean. Are you implying that he let himself out of the office and killed this woman, then came back and waited for me to take him home?"

"Can you give me any information that says he couldn't have done this?"

As it happens, I can. I remember now that I telephoned him about one of his appointments, a little after eleven-thirty. He answered, so he was still in the office."

"We both know that this is nothing more than a pack of lies, don't we?"

"It's true. And I would say this in court if it comes to it."

"Are you in love with your boss, Miss Amuso?"

"That question doesn't deserve a reply. I know Fabio Conti inside out and can tell you that he is incapable of murder. Especially with a knife. It is too personal."

"You know all of the details."

"They are all over the newspaper."

"Did he ever talk to you about Marina Ferro?"

"I am his assistant, not his best friend or lover. We talk about business. We don't have that sort of relationship."

"But you know his reputation as a womanizer."

"I didn't realize that this is now a crime. If that is the case, I can see you having to put most Italian men in prison."

"But you do spend a lot of time with him."

"Now you are acting like a typical Italian, inspector. Just because I spend time with someone, I have to go to bed with him. Maybe when he was younger, I might have been tempted, but Fabio's beauty burned brightly for only a short time. These days he has to pay for the pleasure of young girls and gets his life organized by people like his wife and me. I go with him everywhere; I pay the bills in restaurants, order taxis, and hookers. If he is going to be late home, it is me that has to phone his long-suffering wife and make the excuses.

"You seem to have devoted your life to him. Do you have a family?"

"I get well paid for what I do. Family? Does everybody need to have a spouse or companion? I get by without baggage. I make my own decisions and don't have to ask permission to do anything."

"What about Fabio Conti? Don't you need to ask his permission from time to time?"

"The wonderful thing about our relationship, inspector, is that I do most of the things for him. In a perfect world, I would be able to cut him out and just get the credit myself. I even write his speeches.

It's funny, but I could do without him, but he couldn't do without me."

Visco could see her point, and also felt her frustration. He got up and made his way to the door. "Thank you very much for your time. If I need to speak to you again, I know where to find you."

She didn't get up, but reached for a decanter on the table, and poured herself a drink. It looked like grappa. He could have used a drink at that moment but knew his place. She had been looking down her nose at him as if he was no more than a peasant. Visco had never got used to the way Italian elites did this. It always gave him a feeling of satisfaction when he arrested one, usually for corruption. He didn't feel that corruption was Angela Amuso's particular vice, but he instinctively knew that she must have one, and was determined to find out what it was.

As he drove away from the villa, he decided to make his overdue visit to interview Fabio Conti. He knew that he had left it long enough. However, the message that came through on the car radio changed those plans. He stopped, did a three-point turn and set off in the direction of Lower Maratea and Hugo Berlinski's apartment.

CHAPTER TWELVE

Visco looked around him at the mess in the room. There was an acrid smell of smoke that lingered in the air, and even though the windows were open, it was uncomfortable to breathe. On his arrival, he had found the street in front of the condominium cordoned off, and an ambulance leaving the scene with its siren blaring. His assistant Luca had appeared from out of the main door, and before he could speak, Visco had barked, "Is he dead or alive?"

"Alive but only just. The blade must have missed his heart by a fraction on a millimeter."

"Either that or Berlinski doesn't possess a heart."

"He has lost a lot of blood and is unconscious. The doctor says his chances of surviving are about evens."

Once inside the apartment, his assistant had taken him through the details of what was known.

"What saved him, sir, was an angry neighbor. Apparently, she heard the bumping and banging directly above her from Berlinski's flat and was frightened that it was going to wake her husband up. He is a night shift worker in a bakery. She went upstairs to complain and saw the smoke coming from underneath the door."

"She called the fire brigade?"

"Not at first, she got another neighbor, and they broke the door down and dragged Berlinski out."

"We need to interview this neighbor."

"I am going down in a minute, sir."

"So what do you think?"

"It seems to me that this is linked to the death of Marina Ferro. Whoever did this was looking for something and was disturbed by the neighbor arriving."

"Did the neighbor see anybody leave?"

"Whoever it was left through the kitchen window and went down the fire escape. We are fingerprinting now."

"So they didn't see anybody when they entered the room."

"All that they saw was Berlinski lying unconscious on the floor, covered in blood from a knife wound to the chest."

"I want this place searched. Every centimeter. And I also want a full report off the neighbors and a door-to-door search of all of the houses in the area. You never know, somebody might have seen something. Can we get the backroom boys to give me a fuller report on Berlinski, and throw his fingerprints into the system and see what comes out? I want it as soon as I come back."

"May I ask from where, sir?"

"I'm off to see Fabio Conti. He is very clever, rich and manipulative, or stark raving mad and I intend to find out which."

In the course of his career, Visco had questioned many people, but he always hated celebrities and politicians. In Conti, he had the two rolled into one, which made him doubly apprehensive. His wife said that it was all down to him being an inverted snob. He just didn't like those types of people and felt inferior in their presence. She was probably right, but he was too old to change now.

The street in front of the condominium was quiet and almost deserted. It was late, but the heat from the day lingered, and most Italians were still eating dinner in air-conditioned dining rooms, before going out to mingle in the bars or walk on the seafront. When summer arrived in the south, the evening was the coolest time to be outside, and young and old took advantage. People would start at midnight and continue through the hours that separated night from day. It would be mostly teenagers that made it through until morning, but for many people, an early morning breakfast of coffee and cornetto was the norm, before going home and sleeping through the morning.

The reception was deserted. Pardo had left early. He took the lift up to the top floor and rang the ornate bell of the Conti residence. He could hear footsteps inside, and it was Ana Conti who opened the door. She didn't look surprised to see him.

"You're here to see Fabio."

It wasn't a question but a statement of fact. She led him down a long blissfully cool corridor and into a huge study. The walls were almost entirely covered with books, and the lighting was soft and ambient. Like the corridor, the room was air conditioned and cool.

"Please sit down, inspector. My husband will be with you shortly. He is just finishing off his dinner." She pointed in the general direction of an armchair in front of an oak desk. As she left, Conti came in, and Visco was quick to observe the coldness between them as they passed each other. Maybe Ana Conti wasn't the devoted housewife that she made herself out to be.

Fabio Conti sat down behind his desk and looked at Visco with a bored expression on his face. He looked larger in real life than on the TV screen. His eyes were small dark holes and close together. They examined Visco with curiosity and slight contempt. In the brief moments that he had walked across the room to take his seat, Visco had noticed the swelling stomach that wasn't contained anymore by his trousers, and the stoop in the shoulders that looked like some form of arthritis. This was confirmed by the fingers, which looked swollen and red. The face had obviously been attractive when it was young, but it was now puffy and blotchy and signified too many late nights and too much alcohol. He poured himself a large glass of brandy but didn't offer Visco anything.

Finally, he lit a cigar, leaned back in his chair and blew smoke across the desk.

"I'm rather surprised that it has taken you so long to come and see me, inspector Visco." He spoke with a deep booming voice. The voice of a man used to speaking in public and being listened to. "I am also surprised that you chose to call on my assistant earlier on this evening and ask her questions about me. I could have answered those questions myself. This is highly irregular. Have you been doing your job very long?"

"Long enough, sir. I am assuming that you are referring to me talking to Angela Amuso. She didn't seem that bothered by me visiting her. Did she call you to complain?"

"She called to tell me the questions that you asked. You know of course that I was at a meeting in the Town Hall when Miss Ferro was murdered. That puts me out of the picture of suspects. Wouldn't you agree?"

"I can't agree to anything at this stage. That is why I am here. To ask you some questions about your movement and your relationship with the deceased."

"I was talking to the police commissioner for the region this morning. He is a personal friend of mine. The incident with Miss Ferro came up, and he laughed off any implication of me. Would you like him to ring up your boss to clarify that?"

"If you feel that it will achieve anything, sir." Visco understood what Conti was doing, and it surprised him. Either he was guilty of something, or he just liked trying to frighten people he deemed as beneath him "Is Angela Amuso a close work colleague?"

"I employ Amuso to do all of the tedious tasks that I don't want to do. She told you this. Why ask me something you already know?"

"Is she vital to you doing your job?"

"She likes to think she is, but I could find somebody else tomorrow to do the same work."

"And what about Marina Ferro? What job did she play in your life?"

"I make no excuses for having Miss Ferro on hand. She was an employee, just like Angela Amuso, but she fulfilled a different role."

"I believe that you met her in Naples. Would you like to tell me about it?"

"If you insist. We met at a party, we saw each other a few times after, and I persuaded her to come and live here." He added, "Not that she needed much persuasion. She was having trouble with some unsavory characters in Rome and was glad to be able to escape. Maybe you should be looking there, rather than at me."

"Did you love Marina Ferro?"

"That's a very childish thing to say, inspector. I'm in my sixties and have certain physical needs. These are needs that my wife can't perform. She is happy for me to get them somewhere else."

"So is your wife jealous?"

"My wife is happy to be Mrs. Conti, and have the benefits of what that title provides. She is not jealous in any way. In fact, she is happy for me. I have or rather had, a willing body available to satisfy my sexual needs at any time of the night or day. For that, she was well paid. It worked, inspector, so why would I want to kill her?"

"Did you know about her boyfriend?"

"Barone? I knew about him, but never met him."

"How about you being jealous of him?"

"I admit that I would have preferred him not to have been around, but I wasn't in the least bit bothered."

"Well, you would say that, wouldn't you? Do you think that she loved him?"

"There you go using that word again." He thought about it for a minute and took a sip of his drink. "I have no idea. If she did, then maybe he killed her for sleeping with me. You know what these young Italian men are like. Maybe the thought of me doing what I wanted with his girlfriend got him so angry that he snapped."

"So you admit that you didn't like the fact that she had a younger man in her life?"

"She was a call girl. She slept with anybody who had the money to pay for her. It wasn't as if she was some young virgin that I got tangled up with. Like I have already told you, it was a purely business arrangement. I was paying for a service and nothing more. How was I to know that her life in Rome was going to catch up with her? I repeat; if you want to solve this murder, then you should be looking there and not here. If you want me to get one of your superiors to explain this more clearly to you, then I can assure you I will not hesitate."

Visco stood up and made his way to the door. "It is your choice to do what you see fit, Mr. Conti. I will come back if I need to speak to you further."

When Visco made that last statement, he didn't realize that he would be speaking to Conti in an interview room, within the next two hours. It didn't surprise him because as an old hand at investigating murders, he knew that when they started to unravel it began slowly but speeded up pretty rapidly at the end.

On his return to police headquarters, Luca presented him with the results of the house-to-house search. Apparently, nobody had seen or heard anything. The search of the flat had been a different story, and his men had uncovered a cardboard box under the sink that had been badly burnt in the fire. The cassettes that the box contained had mostly been burned in the fire, but one had barely been touched because it was at the bottom. It was this one that Luca presented to Visco, and it was the reason why Fabio Conti was now sitting across the desk in the interview room.

CHAPTER THIRTEEN

Conti looked as though he had dressed in a hurry, and even though the look of confidence had been maintained on his face, he avoided eye contact and studied his impeccably maintained nails.

Visco switched off the video recorder and sat back in his chair with a smug look on his face. He was enjoying watching the other man's discomfort, though understood that this was not very professional on his part.

"I assume that you recognize both men in this video?"

Conti nodded. "I was drugged by Marina and her boyfriend. It is not what it seems."

"It seems pretty realistic to me. This is a video of you having a sex romp with Hugo Berlinski. Do you have a preference for men or women?"

"I was set up."

"It looks as clear as day to me. Where did this take place?"

"In Rome. It was a threesome with me, Marina and Berlinski. The video has been edited so that it looks as if it is just me and him."

"Why would anybody want to do that?"

"Because it makes me look ...Well, you know what it makes me look like."

"It certainly ruins you masculine image. I am assuming that she was blackmailing you."

"That is correct."

"And you killed her and Berlinski to shut them up."

"That is going to take some proving, Visco. You would never get it to a court of law. I have...."

"Yes, I know. You have friends in high places. Unfortunately, those friends will not want to involve themselves in something like this."

"Like what?"

"Like two murders and a homosexual sex scandal. Why don't you just admit it? You will in the end, so why not save us both the trouble."

"I'm admitting nothing."

"So tell me what happened, at least."

"Marina Ferro is not what you think she is."

"Apparently not."

"She is a manipulating, money grabbing tramp that has been extorting money out of people since she was old enough to have sex."

"So we arrive at the same place. She was extorting money off you, and you decided to kill her."

"I have an alibi for the night she was killed."

"An alibi can be broken if I lean on the right people. You will find that friends and colleagues will only go so far in bending the truth. When it begins to affect them, they will cave in."

"What are you saying?"

"I'm saying that you could have slipped out and walked home during the time you were on your own. We already know that Pardo the doorman is in your pocket and unreliable. In short, you could have killed her."

"I am not a killer. She was blackmailing me, but I negotiated an agreement that suited us both."

"I think you had better tell me about it so that I can decide."

"We did meet at a party in Naples, and I did take her out on a couple of occasions. She charged me, of course, for the pleasure of her body, but at my age, I have got used to that. Then, one night she asked me if I would be interested in a threesome, and that she enjoyed it when two men made love to her. I said OK, so we met for drinks in a hotel that she used, and I was introduced to Berlinski. They must have slipped something into my drink because I can remember very little about the night. A couple of days later she presented me with a cassette tape showing Berlinski and me in bed.

She had been edited out of the whole thing. Of course, we both knew what the consequences were of her going public."

"So she asked you for money."

"You are right, she asked me for an enormous amount of money, but I convinced her that I didn't have any."

"So you lied to her."

"No, I didn't lie. It is the truth. I have been going through a difficult patch and never was that good at saving. I told her that even though I didn't have money I could give her an apartment that was worth more. She wasn't very happy, but she agreed."

"So you are saying that the apartment was signed over to her."

"Discreetly. But yes.

"So why didn't she sell it?"

"She was just about to, then this all happened."

"Yet, you still went down for sex. This seems very strange to me."

"I went down for sex, but still had to pay for it. She was a business woman through and through."

"So, do you have any idea who could have killed her?"

"No."

"What about Berlinski?"

"Her partner? You're the detective. All I can do is repeat that it wasn't me."

Visco concluded the interview just as dawn was beginning to break over the rugged mountains behind Maratea. Professional instinct told him that Conti had, at last, told him the truth. He put out a call to bring in Marina Ferro's boyfriend, Dario Barone. After what had been revealed tonight, he wondered what part, if any, he had played in the blackmail scam.

As he was drinking tepid cappuccino and a bland cornetto in the bar next to the police station, his assistant, Luca, told him that Barone had disappeared. He was back to square one and wondered how his boss would view his progress.

Over a second coffee, he formulated a plan that was so obviously a trap he didn't for a second think it would work. By nine o'clock, he had got Luca to phone up the local radio station, and by nine thirty, he was back in his cramped office looking at the list of possible suspects. Any one of them could have done it, but would one of them be stupid enough to fall for his parlor trick?

CHAPTER FOURTEEN

"The plan worked, sir."

The telephone call had woken Visco up from a troubled sleep. It took him a couple of seconds to focus and remember the plan that Luca was talking about. "What's happened?"

"The plan did work. But there has been a slight snag."

The plan that Luca was referring to involved a police statement that was issued on the local radio and in a couple of local newspapers. Basically, it stated that Berlinski was in a stable condition and when he gained consciousness, would be able to name his attacker. Visco rubbed the sleep from his eyes. "What went wrong?"

"As you said, somebody did try to enter Berlinski's room, but the man we had watching the door made a move too quickly. The attacker managed to push a medicine trolley into him and run away."

"Do we know who the attacker was?"

"No, sir. Whoever it was came dressed as a doctor and had a mask over his or her face. That is what made our man suspicious."

"Don't these people know how to follow instruction? They were told to let whoever came, enter the room and then lock the door. Berlinski was not even in danger. He was in another part of the hospital. So we have lost our attacker."

"Not exactly. Our man did manage to recover and gave chase. The attacker made it all the way to the top floor and is now out on the terrace, standing by the railings. Our men have held back in case the attacker jumps."

"I'm on my way." Visco grabbed his keys, finished off a half cup of cold coffee and ran out of the door.

He burst through the main entrance of the hospital into a dazzle of lights and confusion. He caught the doorframe to steady himself and half closed his eyes. His head felt dizzy due to the lack of sleep and the frantic journey from his house. When he opened them again, Luca was standing in front of him. He turned and led the way towards the lift.

The accident and emergency unit was crowded with tourists. He could tell that they were not local, by their accent. They were mostly Neapolitan or Roman. Within a few seconds of leaving the crowds behind, the lift noiselessly opened its double doors and deposited them on the top floor.

"The terrace is through there," said Luca. He added, I have kept the men back so as not to cause alarm. There is no other way down, so this person is trapped."

"There is another way down, Luca. It's a very quick way, so we will have to be careful. Is there any chance that we could get a net on the floor below just in case our murderer prefers death to life imprisonment?"

"I looked into it, but the floor below is all operating theatres, and they are all in use at the moment."

Visco looked at his watch. It was almost midnight. "At this late hour?"

"Tourists, sir."

"If we can't do it, then I am going to have to use all of my charms." Visco walked slowly down the corridor until he reached the door to the terrace, which was guarded by one of his men. Without stopping to reflect on what course of action he was going to take, he went through the doorway and stood on the dimly lit terrace. The first thing that he noticed was the full moon hanging above the dark sea. It was an idyllic view, with the mountains framed in the backdrop. Underneath the moon was Fabiana Volsi. She was leaning back against the railings looking towards him with a rapturous smile.

She called out, "Hello inspector. I was wondering when you would turn up. It's a beautiful view, don't you think?"

"Hello, Fabiana." He started to move towards the railings. She shook her head ever so slightly, and he stopped.

"Fabiana, there is no need for this."

"Need for what? I am just enjoying the fresh air and the lovely view. It is the best in Maratea. Listen to that silence. Just the sound of the sea, and no Neapolitan tourists with their unwashed kids and fat mothers."

Visco was not trained for situations like this, but he realized that beneath her lightness there was an intense desperation. Whether this desperation was enough to push her over the edge was something he could not fathom out. He said calmly, "It's great, Fabiana, but why don't we go down and grab some coffee or something stronger."

"You seem to be a very nice man, inspector. Can you understand treachery?" She thought about it for a moment and answered her own question. "How foolish of me. You're a policeman. You must deal with treacherous people every day."

"I have met more than my fair share of treacherous people, Fabiana."

"I'm not saying that Marina Ferro deceived me. In a way, I think that I deceived myself. She never told me that she loved me, but I naturally assumed that she did. I was wrong. How could such a gorgeous creature see anything in an old woman like me?"

Visco listened and thought that there was a glimmer of hope that she wouldn't jump. The police manuals that he had read said that once a potential suicide starts talking, then they usually didn't go through with the act. "Do you want to tell me about it?"

She laughed at this and shifted her position against the railings. He wondered if he was close enough to make a grab for her if she tried to jump. With his luck, she would probably pull him over as well.

"You want to know, what a rich, middle-class woman like me, would want to have a relationship with a woman like Marina Ferro?"

"If you want to tell me."

"It's called boredom."

"I don't understand." Visco was determined to keep her talking.

"Look, it's like your acting a part. The perfect middle-class housewife with the same middle-class friends that you see every week. My husband gives me money for what I need, but in return, he expects a certain level of conformity off me. I have a shop, which he bought to keep me occupied during the day, but it's not enough. I have certain needs that can't be satisfied by my husband or his religion crazy friends. For him, the highlight of the week is church on Sunday and inviting the priest back for lunch. For me, it was the time that I spent in bed with Marina. But like everything in my life, Marina let me down."

"How did she let you down, Fabiana?"

"I knew about the financial arrangement that she had with my son-in-law, and I knew about her boyfriend. I assumed that I was more important than both. I assumed wrong."

"So how did you reach this assumption?"

"Marina seduced me. She kept coming into the shop with the excuse that she liked my clothes. I suspected that she didn't and went along with her when she invited me around for coffee. One thing led to another, and we ended up in bed. This was not the first time for me, though my husband is unaware of this."

"So what went wrong in the relationship?"

"That night, I left my daughter, but I didn't go to the car park. I went to see her. She told me to sit down and watch an interesting video. It was me and her. She said that if I didn't start paying her money on a monthly basis, not only was she going to show it to my husband, but she was going to send a copy to all of my friends. I couldn't let her do this, so I killed her with a kitchen knife."

"Ok, I see how upset you must have been, and I am sure that the judges will understand this and go easy on you. It was a crime of anger. Let's go back to the police station and discuss it over coffee."

It was as if she wasn't listening to him. She carried on like he wasn't there. She was trying to justify her actions to herself.

"Of course, if I had thought it all through I would have realized that Marina could not have been operating on her own. It wasn't too long after that night that Berlinski approached me with another copy of the video. This time the price was higher. He was blackmailing me for the murder of Marina as well as my affair with her. What could I do? I arranged to meet him in his apartment and stabbed him. I couldn't find the video, so I tried to burn the place down. I obviously didn't do a very good job. I'm not a very good assassin, am I, inspector?"

"I admit I have met better." He tried another step forward. She didn't seem to notice, but there was still at least twenty feet between them. He could hear the sound of the waves crashing on the beach, and the moon was hidden for a moment behind a small cloud. He thought about making a rush for her. She turned slightly to search for the moon. While she was peering over, he moved forward very slowly.

To turned back and caught him in mid-step. He froze, like as if he was playing the children's game, statues. He smiled sheepishly under her quizzical gaze.

She said, "I like you, inspector." She was no longer looking at him, but even as he tensed up for a sprint, she leaned backward over the railings. With her in this position, he didn't dare to make a move.

"Surely you understand that what you did was what any reasonable person would have done."

She pulled herself back to a standing position, and his pulse returned to a mere seventy percent above average.

"Yes, I suppose you are right. I just could not stand going to prison. I wouldn't survive. Far better a quick end. Do you think it will hurt?"

He could see tears running down her face and a look of despair, as if she realized that she had run out of choices. If he was going to stop her jumping, then it was now that he had to act. He took a large step forward and said with a sense of urgency. "Yes, I think that it will hurt a lot, and you may not even die. Better some nice cozy women's prison for a few years than a wheelchair for life."

"You reckon?" She said. "I can't see me surviving either prison or jumping off this building. Because I have a choice, I think the quick solution looks a lot better. On the other hand, I'm terrified of heights, and the thoughts about falling are just too much. Will you protect me or persecute me, inspector?"

"I'll do my best to help you."

She laughed nervously and moved away from the railings. Visco felt his skin trembling with the relief. He laughed as well and moved towards her.

But even as he laughed and started walking, he knew that he had made a dreadful mistake, by the look that came over her face. He started to run, but he wasn't quick enough. In a fraction of a second, he was standing alone on the terrace. Down below a shrieking noise rose up the sides of the hospital towards the moon that had just appeared again. Visco looked up to the moon and shouted Damn you! He wasn't sure if he was damning Fabiana Volsi or merely himself for not being quick enough.

MURDER REPORT

C281765 (notes to be typed out)

Maratea district of Basilicata, Potenza.

Investigating Officer Inspector Gino Visco

May 15, 1982

The victim, Marina Ferro was stabbed in the throat in her apartment in Maratea. Her background history showed that from a very early age she had been involved in prostitution in Rome, and had been passed around various known pimps in that city.

She was living in her apartment in Maratea, courtesy of politician and TV celebrity, Fabio Conti. We assumed at first that he had set Ferro up in the apartment, in an agreement where she would pay by giving him unlimited sex.

Suspects that we had included Fabio Conte and his wife, Ana. Her boyfriend, Dario Barone. The doorman Filippo Pardo and cleaner Hugo Berlinski were also implicated.

Fabio Conti had an alibi that he was at a meeting. It was proved that in the time that he was alone at the end of the meeting, he could have gone home and murdered Ferro.

His wife Ana had her mother, Fabiana Volsi with her at the time of the murder. Volsi left around eleven.

It was a possibility that doorman Filippo Pardo committed the murder, but I could not find any motive.

Hugo Berlinski was murdered and his apartment partially destroyed by fire. He was killed using a knife, which was different to the one that killed Marina Ferro, but I suspected that the killer was the same person.

We discovered a video showing Fabio Conti having sex with Hugo Berlinski.

I interviewed Conti, and he painted a very different picture of what Marina Ferro was like.

She had set up the video shoot, and it had been edited. It now looked like Conti was having sex just with Berlinski. She was blackmailing him, and the apartment in Maratea was part of the deal.

Hugo Berlinski died of his injuries but was in a coma for several days afterward. I falsely reported to the local radio channels and newspapers that he was making progress and we expected him to reveal his assailant. I had hopes that this would force the hand of the murderer.

In fact, it did cause a reaction, and Fabiana Volsi attempted to kill him while he was in the hospital.

She escaped to the roof terrace of the hospital, and I pursued her. She confessed that she had visited Marina Ferro on the night of the murder. Ferro had tried to blackmail her, and she had killed her in a rage.

She was later contacted by Hugo Berlinski, who also tried to blackmail her. She stabbed him with a knife and failed in her attempt to retrieve the video tape.

Fabiana Volsi threw herself off the roof and died instantly, despite my attempts to talk her down.

In my opinion, Marina Ferro, Hugo Berlinski, and Dario Barone were a team of blackmailers that had worked this scam many times before, in Rome.

Dario Barone told a pack of lies during his interrogation but was extremely convincing. We are still searching for him. I am convinced that he was the camera operator and editor. Upon investigation, we discovered that he did spend a year at the University of Potenza, where he studied filmmaking. The case will close upon his arrest. I do not believe that this man is dangerous, and it will be very difficult to bring charges, as we do not have proof, and all of the witnesses are dead except Fabio Conti. I don't believe that Conti will be too eager to pursue this.

Case concluded.

THE END

Thank you for reading the Inspector Visco.

If you enjoyed it, pass it on and tell some of your friends.

Visit my author page on Amazon: Visit Amazon's John Tallon Jones Page   Click follow, and you will get up-to-date information on all future releases.

Other books by John Tallon Jones:

The Penny Detective Series

1. The Penny Detective

2. The Italian Affair

3. An Evening with Max Climax

4. The Shoestring Effect

5. Chinese Whispers

6. Murder at Bewley Manor

7. Dead Man Walking

8. The Hangman Mystery

Before you go, here is another book by the author

THE PENNY DETECTIVE

WINTER 1985

CHAPTER ONE

I was christened Stanley Morris-Shannon, but only my mum calls me Stanley, and only then when she is ticked off with me. Most other people, including my dad, call me Morris or Moggsy. I'm a private detective, and got into the business by doing what most people do if they are desperate to get a job; I went on a course. The course lasted for a whole four weeks, and the main reason that persuaded me to part with my dad's money to go on it was that I could do most of the studying from home, in between watching afternoon chat shows on TV. The company used a technique that it called distance learning, and what I called a rip-off.

I guess I'm an okay kind of fella though I don't have that many friends. I live in a block of council flats, which suits me down to the ground, though my mum and dad keep telling me that at thirty I should have done better for myself and be married with a couple of kids, and doing a job with regular hours. The fact that dad retired and they moved to the Costa del Sol means that I get less earache. The fact that dad is also a multi-millionaire helps as well because on the allowance he set up for me, I'm not well off, but comfortable enough not to have to do a poxy office job.

I've spent a lot of time living rough in my life, trying to rebel against my public school education, and the family plan to tame the animal inside me enough to carry on the family business. In the end, the life I was leading got too much for even me, and so now, I've given up on the road, and dad has given up trying to change me and sold his used car business. It was mum that made him move to Spain, and it was her that persuaded him to give me an allowance that was not enough for me to kill myself with fast cars and hookers, but sufficient to keep me off the social and pay the rent for my one bedroom bachelor pad.

As a result of an investigation, I was hospitalised last week with suspected concussion and severely bruised ribs; but to be honest, for the most part, my job is nothing out of the ordinary, and can often be quite boring and tedious. This was the first time that I had ever been injured while working, but it was my own fault really. I had been hired to trace a runaway and tracked her down to some waste ground behind the Westhill Housing Estate at the back of the town centre. I thought that I had caught her, but she was a fast runner and agile too because the way she climbed that tree and sat there at the top looking down and daring me to follow, took some guts.

I don't have a head for heights, and for the money I was getting paid, I should have turned around and gone home. For all of the thanks I got for my trouble off the client, I wish I had. I like to see a job through though, so I climbed up, and when I was close enough made a grab for her. She scratched me, but I managed to hold on as we both fell backwards. I ended up severely concussed and wracked with pain on the floor under the tree. Fluffy sat on my chest, licking herself and purring for a couple of seconds, before disappearing into the distance and eventually making her way home.

Most of the jobs I am hired to do aren't as exciting as that one or as dangerous, but from time to time something vaguely interesting happens, and this was the case last week when Karl Ashford dropped by my office. My place of work is not what you would call plush, but the shabbiness has a kind of unique charm that I like and which suits the clientele that pay for my services. I occupy a room above a betting shop on the High Street in Croxley Greater Merseyside. I have an answer phone to pick up my calls when I'm out and to keep the outgoings to a minimum I do my own cleaning and my own accounts.

I was doing the cleaning when Karl walked in on me, and though I had never met him before, I knew of him and his brother and had a pretty good idea what he had come to see me about.

Both Karl and his brother Billy were minor league villains, and, for the most part, contented themselves with dealing in a bit of weed, and some petty thieving. Unfortunately, brother Billy had just got promoted to the First Division and was now on the most-wanted list of the Merseyside Constabulary for murdering his wife's ex- lover, local businessman, Tony O'Brian.

Karl was probably in his late forties, but his lack of hair and grey stubbly pockmarked features made him look a lot older. You got the impression when you were in the same room as him that you were only a couple of words away from getting your head kicked in but, between the two brothers, it was Billy who most locals steered clear of as he had a reputation as a nasty piece of shit. Younger brother

Karl, even though he looked like a gorilla was technically the brains behind the muscle, and rarely resorted to violence. Get on the wrong side of an Ashford, however, and you would eventually end up severely injured, go to bed with the wife of an Ashford, and you more than likely would end up like Tony O'Brian.

I was a bit surprised to see him standing by the door when I turned off the cleaner, and how long he had been there, I couldn't say. The truth is, I would have been surprised to see anyone at that moment as work had been a bit slack, to say the least and, apart from my mate Shoddy dropping by to borrow money to fund his drinking habit, he was the first person to come into the office for a week.

"Are you, Morris Shannon?" he asked looking at the cleaner, then letting his eyes drift around the room. He had the sort of face that didn't give much away about what he was thinking.

"That's me. What can I do for you?" I made a vague hand gesture for him to take a seat.

He sat down and waited for me to wind the lead in, put the vacuum cleaner away in the cupboard and sit down behind my desk.

"You know who I am?" he said

"I know about what happened to your brother if that's what you mean."

"Ok then, so I'll cut out the shit and get to the point. Billy didn't have anything to do with killing O'Brian, and I know that for a fact."

"If you're so sure, then why not go to the police, and save them the trouble of looking for Billy?"

He shook his head and smiled coldly. "I wish it was that simple, Mr Shannon, but what I'm going to tell you is between you and me, and can't go no further." He looked at me before continuing, and I nodded.

"Billy couldn't have set the fire that night because he was robbing a warehouse in Bootle with me."

I repeated my original question. "So what can I do for you?"

"I want you to find out who did kill him, and let me know."

I didn't say anything, hoping that he would fill in the silence with some details that I didn't already know, and was relieved when he obliged.

"The police just want a conviction, and they don't give a damn if it's the right one. Billy is the easy target, and his alibi is a pile of shit, which would put us both away, so you can appreciate the predicament we're in."

"So who do you think killed him?"

"Take your pick; O'Brian was a flash bastard and was no boy scout when it came to making money. There were a few people around here that were happy when he ended up like a roast chicken."

"Including Billy?"

"Billy wasn't bothered either way; he and Clair had what you might call an open marriage, and Billy knew the score and was no angel himself when it came to shacking up with women behind Clair's back. The whole business between O'Brian and Clair happened years ago, so why would Billy do something about it now? Why wait when he could have dealt with it at the time?"

"So where is Billy now?"

"Your guess is as good as mine; he's done a runner, and didn't tell me where he was going. I wish that I knew myself, but that's not important. What is important is to find the bloke that did it so that we can get Billy out of the shit."

"So why choose me, there are bigger agencies in Liverpool?"

Karl shrugged. "Are you telling me you don't need the business?" He looked around the office again and then fixed me with a pair of ice grey eyes.

I needed the business alright; my car needed a service, and the road tax was due. I shoved a form in his general direction as fast as I could, while maintaining steady eye contact.

He filled in his details, then threw a brown envelope at me. "Here are some names of people that you could try for starters and some cash for expenses."

He stood up; we shook hands, and I told him that I would do some work and get back to him when I had something to report. He seemed satisfied by that and let himself out.

CHAPTER TWO

Croxley is not one of the classiest areas on Merseyside; in fact, I would go so far as to say that it is a shit-hole. Just a collection of streets shaded in with damp red brick buildings that have dirty windows and ugly high-rise flats, with a sprinkling of parks, shops, pubs, clubs and Catholic Churches. All street corners come complete with obligatory gangs of jobless scallies, and all roads lead to the M6, and possibly onwards to the M1 and London if you're brave enough. But if you hadn't realised it already, the main drag will take you through the town's boarded up, decaying shopping centre that gives you a definite feeling that life here is at the sharp end of destitution. The only good thing they say to come out of Croxley is the road to the Wirral.

Still; looking on the bright side, there are so many scams, robberies and muggings going on around town that the real police can't cope, and they have given up trying, so there is plenty of work for a good private detective, which I wish I was. You could say that I am in the right place at the right time with the wrong skills. Before Karl had walked through my door and thrown money at me, I was thinking of jacking it in, getting another loan from my dad and opening a fish and chip shop.

I left the office a couple of minutes after Karl, having waited with my coat on to give him time to clear the stairs. As I walked along the High Street, I racked my brains for what I knew about the murder of O'Brian. Funnily enough, I used to work for him a few years ago, as a doorman in one of his clubs. Back then, I had long hair and just about got away with this line of work without serious injury because I am six feet four. This tended to put the drunks off having a pop at me, but people told me that my face was just too sweet looking to be a proper bouncer. It was during my time working for O'Brian that I had a brainwave, shaved my hair off and developed a menacing leer. This seemed to do the trick with most punters. In those days, I was the master of the vice-like grip around the top of the arm, and a quiet word if trouble started. This usually meant I kept my tuxedo a blood free zone, which saved on the dry cleaning bills. I never did grow my hair back, and I'm still developing variations of that menacing sneer.

I never met O'Brian to speak to but didn't need a one on one with him to realise what he was about. I always put his aggressive streak down to the fact that he was very small with red hair. Even when I was working for him, he was known as a bit of a bad lad who didn't mind getting rough if he couldn't do it the friendly way. He'd managed to get a fair size business together, with a couple of clubs, some betting shops, and flats that he rented out to students and low-life. There were always rumours about the man flying around the streets, especially about how he had started off his empire by running a protection racket. Businesses in the area would pay him money every month to avoid getting their premises burnt. It smacked a little bit of ironic justice to me seeing how he had died with his hands tied behind his back in a fire.

Whoever had killed him and for whatever reason, I doubted that there would be many tears shed for the guy. At fifty-five, with at least twelve years of making enemies in Croxley alone, the Sharks would already be assembling ready to divide up his business interests, many of which were now totally legit.

The night he died, from what I could remember from the local newspaper, he was last seen at around midnight in one of his clubs called the Oasis. He'd got a phone call and left in a hurry, and then neighbours reported smoke and flames coming out of his house at around four in the morning. By the time the fire brigade lads could get inside, all that remained of the poor bastard was charcoal, but it was later found out that his hands had been tied, and his head smashed in with something akin to a sledgehammer.

The reason Billy's name came up so quickly was because of information given to the police from an anonymous source. The reason Billy managed to escape out of the back door of his house was that the police, in their wisdom, arrived with sirens blazing in the early hours of the morning. They could just as easily have sent him a letter, asking if he could be in when they called, and I guessed that the chief inspector who had cocked this one up was getting some earache off his boss and was probably back on traffic duty.

This all happened about a month ago, and Billy has not been seen since. The press picked up the story of Billy's wife Clair being the ex-lover of O'Brian, again, through an anonymous call, though the police didn't confirm or deny it officially. That's the crappy thing about living in Croxley. Everybody wants to know your business, and there is very little you can get away with without someone finding out and passing it around. The only people that didn't seem to have a clue at what was going on in Croxley were the police. The official reason for Billy being number one suspect had not been released, though the fact that he ran away didn't look good.

My flat is on the second floor of a high-rise complex that was condemned as unfit for human habitation twenty years ago and is only a twenty-minute walk from my office. The lift very rarely works and when it does, it gives you the impression that it won't be working for long. You feel grateful when the doors eventually open, and you are free to leave and carry on your life. The two-floor climb I write off as my daily workout, and today I did the stairs two at a time, before arriving wheezing and red-faced at the door of my next door neighbour and best friend, Shoddy.

The figure that opened it and let me in was a curious mix to look at. To someone that didn't know him, Shoddy would more than likely be written off as a bum. I could smell the cider in the air as he led me through to his combined lounge and kitchen and as I sat down, he cleared a couple of empty cans of Special Brew into the waste basket and poured me a glass of cheap Bulgarian Cider.

Shoddy is in his late forties with a face that has a derelict aura. There are bags under the bags of his washed-out blue eyes, and his grey receding hairline and lack of teeth is finished off nicely by nicotine stained fingers and a permanent odour of ready- rubbed tobacco and cheap booze.

The man looked as if he belonged in a shop doorway sleeping under a pile of newspapers, and sometimes it was hard even for me to believe that when I first met him, he was a top-cop that was on his way to a position in the higher echelons of the Merseyside Police Force. Drink and heroin addiction stopped all that, and he was relieved of his post on the grounds of ill health, after trying to kill himself with Paraquat. The pressure had somehow got to him, and he had never told me the reason it all turned bad, but it must have been something pretty heavy.

These days the bags of heroin are a distant memory, and he contents himself with blocking out reality with strong cider for breakfast and cheap cans of supermarket lager. But you would be a fool to think that Shoddy was a vegetable even though he often smelt like one. He had the sharpest mind of anyone I have ever known, and still had some good police contacts, who remembered what he once had been. For me, he was the ideal person to do all of the boring detail work that was a big part of being a private detective, and the best part of our working relationship was that he worked for tobacco and booze.

I sat in an old armchair, and he settled on the settee across from me and started rolling a cigarette. "What's up, Moggsy? You're not usually home this early."

"What would you say if I told you I got a visit from Karl Ashford a bit ago, and he gave me money to prove that brother Billy was innocent?"

That certainly stopped him rolling; well, only for a couple of seconds. As he picked a bit of tobacco out of his cigarette and put it in his tin; without looking at me, he said, "I hope you threw it back at him and told him where to go."

"Work is work, mate, and we haven't had too much lately."

He lit his cigarette, shook his head, and spit out a piece of tobacco. "It's cut and dried as far as I can see, he was caught shagging an Ashford, and they killed him. That's what they do. It smells of trouble to me, and I think you'd be an idiot to get involved. Let the police sort it out. Even they can't make a hash of this one, and it's just a matter of time before they get him."

"We shook hands. I've already agreed to take the case."

He shrugged. "So what's the deal, Moggs?"

"He gave me some names for starters, but what I want is some more background information on O'Brian. Dig around and see if he has upset anybody recently, or find out who would have benefitted from him being dead."

I knew from the look on his face that he thought I wanted my head examining, and probably also thought like I did that I was out of my depth on this one. But if there was one thing that you could count on with Shoddy, it was that he would go along with you, even if he didn't agree with what you were doing.

"I'll poke a few contacts with my stick and see what comes up, but it's gonna cost. How much did he give you?"